# Mutabilitie

Frank McGuinness was born in Buncrana, Co. Donegal, and now lives in Dublin and lectures in English at University College, Dublin. His plays include *The Factory Girls* (Abbey Theatre, Dublin, 1982), *Baglady* (Abbey, 1985), *Observe the Sons of Ulster Marching Towards the Somme* (Abbey, 1985; Hampstead Theatre, London, 1986), *Innocence* (Gate Theatre, Dublin, 1986), *Carthaginians* (Abbey, 1988; Hampstead, 1989), *Mary and Lizzie* (RSC, 1989), *The Bread Man* (Gate, 1991), *Someone Who'll Watch Over Me* (Hampstead, West End and Broadway, 1992) and *The Bird Sanctuary* (Abbey, 1984). His translations include Ibsen's *Rosmersholm* (RNT, 1987), *Peer Gynt* (Gate, 1988; RSC and international tour, 1994), *Hedda Gabler* (Roundabout Theatre, Broadway, 1994) and *A Doll's House* (West End and Broadway, 1997); Chekhov's *Three Sisters* (Gate and Royal Court, London, 1990) and *Uncle Vanya* (Field Day Productions, 1995); Lorca's *Yerma* (Abbey, 1987); Brecht's *The Threepenny Opera* (Gate, 1991) and *The Caucasian Chalk Circle* (RNT, 1997); and Sophocles' *Electra* (Donmar Warehouse, London, 1997).

*by the same author*

# FRANK MCGUINNESS

# Mutabilitie

*faber and faber*
LONDON · BOSTON

First published in 1997
by Faber and Faber Limited
3 Queen Square London WC1N 3AU

Typeset by Faber and Faber Ltd
Printed in England by Mackays of Chatham plc, Chatham, Kent

A CIP record for this book
is available from the British Library

ISBN 0-571-19342-0

2 4 6 8 10 9 7 5 3 1

*For Theresa Nolan*

# Characters

**Edmund**, an English poet in the service
of the English crown
**Elizabeth**, his wife
**William**, their visitor
**File**, their Irish servant, a bard
**Hugh**, their Irish servant, son to Sweney
**Children** to Edmund and Elizabeth
A king, **Sweney**, a dispossessed Irish chieftain
**Maeve**, his queen
**Annas**, his daughter
**Niall**, his son
**Donal**, his priest
**Ben**, their English captive
**Richard**, their English captive

**Mutabilitie** was first performed at the Cottesloe Theatre, Royal National Theatre, London, on 14 November 1997 with the following cast:

**Ben**  Kevin Doyle
**Richard**  James Buller
**William**  Anton Lesser
**The File**  Aisling O'Sullivan
**Edmund**  Patrick Malahide
**Hugh**  Peter Gowen
**Elizabeth**  Diana Hardcastle
**Sweney**  Gawn Grainger
**Maeve**  Frances Tomelty
**Donal**  Sean Campion
**Niall**  Conor McDermottroe
**Annas**  Alison McKenna

*Directed by*  Trevor Nunn
*Designed by*  Monica Frawley
*Lighting by*  Andrew Bridge
*Music by*  Shaun Davey
*Movement by*  Jane Gibson

# Act One

## SCENE ONE

*A patch of light in a forest.*

**Ben** This is Ireland. We are in it. We are alive, breathing the air of Ireland, unknown, unwanted and unloved. The air though is sweet, so maybe it bids us welcome. I love air, don't you? Where would we be without it?

**Richard** Dead.

*William groans loudly.*

I think William is dying.

**Ben** I think William deserves to die. He brought us here.

*There is a faint beat of drums.*

Oh dear, is that thunder? That's all we need. William sick, you sulking, and now rain. It rains a lot in Ireland.

**Richard** It didn't rain last night. It should have.

**Ben** Taking an axe to the stage was a bit much. Really, I was prepared for the passionate Irish, and I can handle a rowdy audience, but I am not prepared to sacrifice my life –

*The drumbeats intensify.*

It's definitely thunder.

*The drumbeats grow deafening. They stop suddenly. Strange sounds are heard. William rises and listens.*

**Richard** What the hell is this? What's happening?

*William starts to stumble towards the river.*

**Ben**  Feeling a bit better, William?

*William falls into the river. The drumbeats return deafeningly. Ben and Richard cling to each other. The clearing darkens. Hooded figures drag Ben and Richard apart.*

**Richard**  Ben.

**Ben**  Richard.

**Richard**  In the name of Jesus, let us go.

**Ben**  Let me go, for Christ's sake.

**Ben**  Where is William? He's deserted us.

**Richard**  William, save us.

*Ben and Richard are dragged away. The drums cease.*


### SCENE TWO

*Music. The File and Hugh wander through the landscape. Edmund and his children follow them tentatively. The File sings.*

**File**
And a man shall come from a river,
He shall gleam like a spear, like a fish,
He shall kill and he shall feed us,
He shall lie and he shall heed us,
He shall give us the gift of tongues,
He shall do nor say nothing rash
But shall sing the song of all songs,
And a man shall come from a river.

Bard meaning poet,
River meaning aibhne,
Bard meaning poet,
River meaning aibhne.

2

*The File sees a bundle of clothes in the water.*

Master, master, master.

*Hugh drags a man from the river. He pumps water out of him, choking. Edmund watches. The File stands behind him, a child in each hand.*

**Child**  Is he drowned, father?

**Edmund**  Be quiet, child.

*The man coughs violently.*

**Child**  Is he a monster, father?

*The man continues to cough.*

Peace be to you, good monster, in the name of God trouble us no more.

**Hugh**  He is alive, master.

*Edmund goes and holds the man's face. The man weeps.*

**Edmund**  I am an Englishman. I am Edmund. Despite your ragged clothing I know you are a civilized man.

*The man buries his head in Edmund's embrace, weeping.*

An Englishman. A civilized man. Gentle brother, rest you. Bring him to the castle.

*Edmund and the children leave. The man sits out the words.*

**Man**  Praise God and his blessed mother. Blessed virgin mother, Lady most pure, most immaculate, tower of ivory, pearl of Christ.

*The File and Hugh look at each other.*

3

*Hugh cuts wood with an axe. The File collects wood already cut. Edmund sits in his study. The blow of an axe.*

**Edmund** It is not with Ireland as it is with most countries, where the wars flame most in summer, and the helmets glisten brightest in the fairest sunshine. But in Ireland the winter yieldeth best services, for then the trees are bare and naked, which used to both clothe and house the kerne; the ground is cold and wet, which used to be his bedding; the air is sharp and bitter to blow through his naked sides and legs; the kyne are barren and without milk, which used to be his only food.

*The blow of an axe. Edmund goes towards Hugh and the File.*

God bless the work.

*They smile at him. Hugh bows, signalling to the File to do likewise. She does.*

Your good woman has the strength of a man.

**Hugh** That she does.

**Edmund** And are you content inside the castle, both of you?

**File** Safer here, sir, than outside.

**Edmund** We are proud of you, my wife and I.

**File** Proud?

**Edmund** Elizabeth tells me you have accomplished much.

**File** Your lady wife is kind.

**Edmund** I will not detain you from your work. (*He turns to leave them, stops.*) Does our English visitor recover?

**Hugh** He has still not spoken like a man of reason. He babbles, but he sleeps soundly.

**Edmund** You attend to him kindly?

**File** Most kindly.

**Hugh** Sir?

**Edmund** Yes, Hugh?

**Hugh** You will not forget to tell us the remainder of the story? The story of the courteous heroes, the knights, the soldiers of the great King Arthur?

**File** And the virgin, the holy virgin, the fairy queen?

**Edmund** I think the story may have ended.

**File** Why?

**Edmund** I have told myself enough of it.

**File** But we still have not heard enough of the queen. Who is she?

**Hugh** She is like a child, looking forward to it.

**File** Is she beautiful?

**Edmund** Yes.

**File** And jewelled?

**Edmund** Yes.

**File** Does her dress weigh her down? All lace and silk?

**Edmund** Lace and silk, yes. Shall I tell you of the queen? Sit.

*Hugh and File sit at Edmund's feet.*

She is the fairest creature to tread God's earth. All who look at her do so with awe and obedience.

**File**  Awe.

**Hugh**  And obedience.

**Edmund**  Beams of light spread from her like the sun's rays. When she speaks, the birds of the air sing to her accompaniment. When she walks, flutes sound through the air.

*Music.*

And she herself of beautie soveraigne Queene
Fair Venus seemed unto his bed to bring
Her, whom he waking evermore to weene.
To be the chastest flowre, that ay did spring
On earthly braunch, the daughter of a king.

In her eyes lie the most precious jewels of all, for they are the mirror of her soul, and it shines like the most beautiful diamond. This is Gloriana. Elizabeth.

*The File and Hugh whisper.*

**File**  Elizabeth.

**Hugh**  Gloriana.

**Edmund**  This is the queen I serve, and whom you long to see.

*The music ceases.*

It is a good longing, for it reflects upon your soul, a soul worth saving. For the sake of your soul I would continue with all my heart the story of this fairy queen, but my sickness forbids me.

**File**  May I ask of your sickness?

6

**Hugh**  She may help you, sir, in your sickness.

**Edmund**  Help?

**Hugh**  She is learned.

**Edmund**  In what?

**Hugh**  The ways of our people. She is called the File. It means wise. She is instructed in poetry and –

**File**  And in magic.

**Hugh**  Law and languages.

**File**  Magic. And magic only. What law do we have to speak of but that of the forest? What language but the growling of a dog? What poetry could we create for the glory of God? Sir, I am knowledgeable only in magic.

**Edmund**  Are you a witch?

**File**  What is a witch?

**Edmund**  An evil woman.

  *Silence.*

**File**  What is evil?

  *Silence.*

**Edmund**  This magic is not magic. It is the legacy of your faith in Rome. Its spells and charms you must renounce. It is not learning. It is ignorance. You must cease to believe in it, as you have ceased to believe in your faith.

**Hugh**  It is in your story, magic.

**Edmund**  That is simply a story. Something to be told and marvelled at, but not to be believed in.

**File**  Is that why it has stopped, your story?

  *Silence.*

7

**Edmund**  Have you heard me speak of awe and obedience? (*Silence.*) Have you?

**Hugh**  Yes.

**Edmund**  Do I feed you and clothe you?

**Hugh**  Yes.

**Edmund**  Do I beat you?

**File**  No.

**Hugh**  No.

**Edmund**  Is that why you love me? (*Silence.*) Do I treat you as my children? (*Silence.*) Do I?

**Hugh**  Yes.

**Edmund**  To remain safe in this castle, there is one rule to obey. You have proved yourselves to be good, obedient creatures. I see in your behaviour the benevolent future of your unfortunate Irish race. You have proved yourselves capable –

*Elizabeth enters, interrupting.*

**Elizabeth**  No, they have proved themselves capable of nothing. They've fooled you. She watches me for any chance to steal from me. He would lay hands upon me if he didn't fear your anger. They are of one breed with those beyond these walls. They will destroy us all, given time. They will find their time. You are mad to retain them, Edmund. Send them out where they belong beyond these walls to live as animals live.

**Edmund**  Elizabeth, my loved wife –

**Elizabeth**  Save your honeyed words. If you loved me, you would rid my home of vermin. You devote your every hour to the taming of these savages –

8

**Edmund**  They now speak our language –

**Elizabeth**  They could when they arrived. How else could they have learned so early to lie with such excellence?

**Edmund**  They listen –

**Elizabeth**  To you and you to them. But you don't hear the whispers, plotting behind your back. These innocents, these children –

**Edmund**  Work hard for us. I am pleased by their hard work. I thank them for it. I reward their intelligence –

**Elizabeth**  Intelligence?

**Edmund**  They are intelligent beings. They are capable of instruction. They are capable of salvation.

**Elizabeth**  They are animals.

*Edmund roars at her.*

**Edmund**  They are Irish.

*Silence.*

**Elizabeth**  You share my fear.

**Edmund**  Be quiet, Elizabeth.

**Elizabeth**  In your heart you are afraid of them.

**Edmund**  I have asked you to be quiet.

**Elizabeth**  You have seen the devastation of these late wars of Munster. They are seeking revenge against us.

**Edmund**  No more.

**Elizabeth**  We are scarcely protected.

**Edmund**  No more.

**Elizabeth**  And they are in our midst. You have seen what has been done. How could they do anything but hate us? As we must hate them.

**Edmund** They are civilized. I have succeeded in that. Perhaps in that alone, but I have succeeded. From that I draw strength. Say you are right, say the castle is surrounded and we must flee. These you would be rid of may be the saving of us in London. They are proof we may succeed in this accursed island.

**Elizabeth** Accursed?

**Edmund** The blessings of our Saviour brought to them through our queen and her ambassadors shall render this island no longer accursed.

**Elizabeth** And if that fail? (*Silence.*) Do we kill them all and thereby succeed? Do we kill them all? (*Silence.*) Kill them all. I have heard that fear in the beating of your heart.

**Edmund** You no longer hear my heart.

**Elizabeth** Be rid of them.

**Edmund** To where? To certain death? No.

**Elizabeth** Then be rid of me.

**Edmund** To lose you I do fear above all else. (*Silence.*) Our duties in this country are manifold. We are here at the behest of our sovereign. We must win this people to England's law, to England's custom, to her religion. If we fail, then we abandon this lost people to the devil. This conquest does not depend on the sword or the scabbard but on our souls, and if we keep faith with the almighty God whose destiny we praise and follow, then we shall win the Irish to our cause. My love, my wife, it is a just cause, this Protestant cause, it is a great one. Let me keep my courage and my faith, Elizabeth. Let me start at least in this their conversion. Let me persist. And help me, as is your duty.

**Elizabeth** Some morning I shall wake as others have before, and my husband, you shall be lying dead beside me, and I will weep for you, as is my duty, since you could not defend me, indeed would not defend me, as is your duty. You have work to do, Edmund. As I have work to do. As they have. Pray, let us continue working, together, in this unhappy home. (*Elizabeth leaves.*)

**Edmund** She suffers. She misses England.

**File** Is she like Elizabeth the queen? Is the queen cruel?

**Edmund** Cruel? (*Edmund laughs.*) No, she is gentle.

**Hugh** Like you.

**Edmund** Gentle, me? Not always. Not in the service of my queen. Go back to work.

*Edmund returns to his study. Hugh resumes his work. The File watches him.*

**File** You spoke too highly of my learning.

**Hugh** I have planted a seed.

**File** This may not be the right season.

**Hugh** I shall decide on the seasons, and you shall obey them.

**File** I have ceased to obey you, Hugh.

**Hugh** I have ceased to love you.

**File** Aye, our duty is no longer to each other. It is to our race. Remember that, Hugh.

*They laugh lowly. A blow of the axe. Elizabeth enters, and lays her hands on Edmund's shoulders.*

**Edmund**  Had I not saved them, Elizabeth, how could they save themselves? They cried at my door like animals, begging for food and shelter. With hard restraint have they not proved themselves to be useful animals? I have saved them. Rejoice. Have they and you and I not seen these late wars of Munster?

*The blow of an axe. During Edmund's speech the axe falls at intervals, the blows rising to a crescendo at its conclusion.*

The same province of Munster was a most rich and plentiful country, full of corn and cattle, that you would have thought they should have been able to stand long, yet before one year and a half, they were brought to such wretchedness, as that any stony heart would have rued the same. Out of every corner of the woods and glens they came creeping forth upon their hands for their legs could not bear them. They looked like anatomies of death, they spoke like ghosts crying out of their graves, and if they found a plot of watercress or shamrocks, there they flocked as to a feast for the time, yet not able long to continue therewithal; that in short space there were none almost left, and a most populous and plentiful country suddenly left void of man and beast; yet sure in all that war, there perished not many by the sword, but all by the extremity of famine, which they themselves had wrought, in these late wars of Munster.

*The axe falls. During Edmund's speech the Irish aristocracy appears.*

### SCENE FOUR

*The forest. A king, Sweney, and his queen, Maeve, preside over the remnants of their court. Their priest, Donal, sits*

*near them. Their son, Niall, watches his parents. Their
daughter, Annas, prepares food. Two captive Englishmen,
Ben and Richard, are gagged and bound together. The File
entertains the company.*

**File** And so he believes we shall all perish, by hunger. I do
begin to imagine it troubles his conscience. Even if he
would dismiss our ways as those of a savage, he yet sees
in our savagery some pain of humanity which has not
been starved out of us. Hugh and I still play the idiot. I
even had him believe I did not know the meaning of evil. I
told him I could work magic. He asked if I were a witch.

**Maeve** And your reply?

**File** I asked, what is a witch?

**Maeve** And he answered?

**File** An evil woman.

**Maeve** Your defence?

**File** What is evil?

**Maeve** Perfect.

*She kisses her husband, the king.*

Our wise woman is amongst them, my husband. She
knows every entrance to their castle. She has convinced
the fools she is their loyal servant. But she comes in secret
to serve us. She can move through this landscape in deep-
est darkness, knowing it is her own. Our own taken from
us. This Edmund, his breeding if you please, my File.

**File** I believe he may be what the English call a bastard. A
son born out of wedlock. Wedlock means marriage. It is
appropriate for them, for they lock their women up. A
savage race. The power of any civilization depends on the
potency of its women.

**Maeve**  They do have a queen.

**File**  It is said she would discard her petticoats in the morning if she felt by so discarding, she would also lose her most precious jewel, and all to be a man. A woman who would be a man. And why? To be King of England.

**Maeve**  I shall never understand them.

**File**  The English?

**Maeve**  Women. They cannot be happy. It is a mystery to me. My sex. They seem born to be unhappy. And without happiness, what is there?

**Donal**  Good Queen, do not remember a time of happiness.

**Maeve**  Would to God I could not remember.

**Donal**  Does she believe in God, this English woman, their queen?

**File**  Good priest, God is so important to this English people they have declared their queen to be his representative on earth. God has moved from the heavens and taken his lodgings in London. Elizabeth is his landlady. Naturally such a distinguished guest requires certain demands, not least a profound self-importance from those who believe in him. Elizabeth announces her virginity to the world and proclaims it to be a sacred decree. So sacred that when she lies with a man, as she must, she does not offer him her jewel for pleasure, she offers instead –

*Maeve laughs.*

As if she, the virgin could give birth through –

**Maeve**  She will, she will.

**Sweney**  This is the talk of vulgar women.

14

**File**  My lord, I beg forgiveness.

**Niall**  She and Hugh have entered the Englishman's castle. They have become his trusted servants. She serves us well, father.

**Sweney**  Sing for me, good poet.

*The File sings.*

**File**
Before Christ died, your father's fathers lived,
Your sons and daughters rule the earth,
Your name be blessed in holy Heaven,
May ye know neither pain nor dearth.

*Annas and Niall join singing with the File in chorus.*

**Chorus**
I have sung your praise for centuries,
Your name is sweet as Saviour,
I have charmed ice winds as they freeze,
Here sweet breezes I have lured.

**Sweney**  My son.

*Niall goes and kisses his father's bare feet.*

My daughter.

*Annas goes and kisses her father's bare feet.*

**Annas**  I beg favour from my father.

**Sweney**  Ask, good daughter.

**Annas**  Father, my lord, I weep for our captives. All night I hear them moan! Their sorrow hurts my heart. Let both be released, let them both go.

**Sweney**  Where? Into the darkest forest? That would be cruel, Annas. They would be lost for ever without our protection. Here, they are safe. They have milk to drink

15

and berries to eat. We share our plenty with them.
Without our kingly generosity they would surely starve to
death. You have seen the starving of your own people. Do
you wish them to die in so hideous a fashion?

**Annas** I do not.

**Sweney** Your tender heart endears you to me. Let it never
grow too hard.

**Maeve** Let it not remain too tender.

**Sweney** You may remove the cloth from one of their
mouths.

*Annas takes the gag from Richard's mouth.*

**Richard** God in heaven, hear her. Have you the power to
hear? Save us. William who led us to this island, to this
forest, lead us now from it. God, hear us.

**Annas** He is praying, father. God will hear him.

**Richard** Let us not be killed, good girl. God, help us.

*Maeve violently gags Richard's mouth.*

**Maeve** What fools these English are. They cry to God as
if their cries will be heard. When we cried, we heard only
the sky answer us in silence, for the very sky is now the
queen of England's.

**Donal** My sovereign lady, you are blaspheming –

**Maeve** Is it blaspheming to tell the truth? Is it blaspheming to believe in hell? What else have we left to believe in?

*Silence.*

**Annas** A man will come amongst us. He will be from a
river. The water shall save him. The river shall reveal him.
He shall speak our stories. A man shall come from the
river. That is the prophecy of the File.

**File**  The man is here. He is with them. I found him in the river. He is not beautiful. But he is a believer. Thinking he was breathing his last, he called out to the Holy Virgin. The Blessed Virgin! The fool Edmund convinced himself he was calling to the fairy queen. Your son, Hugh, attends to him, my lord. Your son shall learn everything.

**Annas**  Then we are saved? (*Silence.*) This man shall save us? Has the File not prophesied –

**File**  Yes.

**Annas**  And your prophecy is true?

*Silence.*

**Maeve**  What is troubling you? He is of our faith.

**File**  Yes, but he is an Englishman. He is an Englishman, who is of our faith.

*The File sings.*

And a man shall come from a river,
He shall gleam like a spear, like a fish,
He shall kill and he shall feed us,
He shall lie and he shall heed us,
He shall give us the gift of tongues,
He shall do nor say nothing rash,
But shall sing the song of all songs,
And a man shall come from a river.

Bard meaning poet,
River meaning aibhne,
Bard meaning poet,
River meaning aibhne.

*Silence.*

He is an Englishman. The man who will sing the song to save us is English. (*She points to Richard.*) He is the

William our captive called out to. Who is he? (*She removes the gag from Richard's mouth*.)

**Richard**  May he rot in hell before he answers you.

**File**  And may you. (*She regags him.*)

# Act Two

## SCENE ONE

*The castle. William lies, fevered, drenched in sweat on straw. Hugh kneels beside him, drying him clean. The File watches them both.*

**William**  The buds grow in the summer.

**Hugh**  They do.

**William**  In May the buds grow golden in my father's garden. In the summer. My father took a lease on his life. It was too short, my father's life. The date of his death, the day was too hot. The eye of heaven looked on him, and he who shone like gold dimmed into death on the day of a fair, they say. He declined. I chanced to be away from home. I thought he was eternal, eternal, he would not fade. In summer, a fair day, my father lost possession of what he owned. The day turned to shade. Eternal father. He said to me, you are a blaggard. You will come to no good in your wandering. Mark my words. Can you breathe, man? Can you see, eyes? Live – give life, my father said. Too hot, more lovely. Chance, changing, eternal. My father said I was a blaggard. I let the fox get at the geese.

**Hugh**  No harm done, no harm done.

**William**  I let the fox get at the geese.

**Hugh**  They can't help it. That's their nature. Don't work yourself up.

*William lies in Hugh's arms.*

You're not too bad, not bad-looking. All right, William.

That's your name. William. Do you remember that? You told us that. You remembered your name was William. You're an Englishman. You're in Ireland. Do you know that? My name is Hugh.

**William** William, Hugh.

**Hugh** You're taking that much in? I am an Irishman. You are English. We are friends. I will not hurt you. Do you remember what happened to you? (*Silence.*) Do you not remember? (*Silence.*) Are you a soldier?

**William** I have been.

**Hugh** Who did you fight for?

**William** I have also been a king and his queen and a boy and his girl and a lover and a clown, all these trades come naturally to me when I sit alone and sometimes I hear sweet airs in the fire, throw water on the fire, let the ashes sing – (*William sings.*) Dig the grave, dig the grave – (*Silence.*) I can't remember what I am. I don't know. (*He starts to clap his hands.*)

**Hugh** What are you doing?

*William continues clapping. He stops suddenly.*

**William** I can't remember. Who is master in this house?

**Hugh** The master is kind and gentle here.

**William** You are not the master?

**Hugh** No, he is an Englishman, like yourself. When you're a bit better, he'll question you. He'll look after you. I'm looking after you now.

**William** I like that.

**Hugh** I know you do.

**William** How do you know that, Hugh?

**Hugh** William, I know.

**William** William.

**Hugh** Hugh.

**William** English.

**Hugh** Irish. That's the man.

*William goes to touch Hugh. Hugh holds both
William's hands gently.*

No, no.

*Edmund enters.*

**Edmund** How does he fare?

**Hugh** Master, I cannot follow him. His mind and tongue
are not as one. His words dart from glen to river.

**Edmund** You have discovered nothing more.

**Hugh** Nothing, but that his father died at a fair day. It
was in the summertime. The father considered him to be a
blaggard. So he has been babbling, like a child.

**Edmund** William, why have you come amongst us?
(*Silence.*) Where have you come from and why? (*Silence.*)
What were you looking for? Was there anyone with you?
Can you tell us? (*Silence.*) Can you tell us if there was
more than one of you? What happened to you, William?

**William** We walked on foot, into a forest where all life
seemed to have left. No birds sang. We watched the
ground and all above us to save ourselves from the savages but they fell on us and bit our flesh like wolves. I
thought they would have pierced my heart and drank my
blood. There were men and women upon us. I don't
remember. Save us, father in heaven.

**Edmund** Us? How many of you were there?

21

**William** Two are captives. I broke free and ran. I am tired.

**Edmund** Are they Englishmen, the captives?

*Silence.*

**William** Yes. English.

**Edmund** Why did you risk coming to this country?

**William** To play.

**Edmund** He babbles again.

**Hugh** Play what?

**William** To play our parts upon the stage. To receive due reward. To live like lords in Ireland. To meet the poet Edmund. To plead my case before him. To take me into his service, that I may cease playing for I am tired of this theatre. Come with me to Ireland. My friends, I have so plotted my destiny that there shall be plenty for us all in Ireland. Follow me, dear friends. I am tired. (*He claps his hands.*) Tired. I remember.

**Edmund** My dear servants, how subtle is the instrument of the human mind. So delicate in its reasoning, so dainty in its imagining. It is yet God's great gift and God's great curse. How the soul of man can suffer through the mind diseased. Minister to him gently. Stay with him, one of you. Remember whatever else he may say, the queen herself may have sent him. William, when I first set eyes on you, beyond this castle, in the name of pity, I showed you mercy, poor soul, suffering. I will open my door and my heart to you, even if I must close them shut against so many. My heart is as heavy in sorrow, William, as yours is deep in distress that I cannot save all beyond these walls as I have saved you and these my servants. They wash away your fever with water as they have been washed in

22

the waters of Our Lord. Let that same divine water wash this country clean. Convert it to the true faith of Jesus Christ Our Saviour from whom all revelation and redemption spring forth eternally at the behest alone of our divine sovereign Elizabeth of England. Most gracious virgin, lady most pure, lady immaculate, tower of ivory, pearl of Christ, your soldiers guard your chastity in this pagan country where Rome and its legions of priests and heathens would violate the sacred bed of England. Shower thy mercy on your most lowly, obedient servant. Hear my prayer, my virgin Queen, Elizabeth, guide me in righteousness. Guide these my servants in goodness. Guide this, our stranger, William, to thy eternal truth. And this country of Ireland, let your blessings rain upon its rivers. Cleanse it of herself. Cleanse it of Rome. Reform it to the true faith. I ask this in God's name. Amen.

**Hugh** Amen.

*Edmund exits.*

Why did you not say amen?

**File** I did not think it polite to listen to the Protestant at prayer. My dear William, are you asleep? I require you to be awake. I require your eloquence. Tell me, William, about this summer's day you were babbling about. (*She is now lying beside William.*) Speak prettily, my loved William. We must lift the odour of Edmund Spenser. Outwit him, William, my Papist, my pupil, my Englishman. Who are you?

**William** (*whispers*)
   Shall I compare thee to a summer's day?
   Thou art more lovely and more temperate.
   Rough winds do shake the darling buds of May,
   And summer's lease has all too short a date.
   Sometimes too hot the eye of heaven shines,

And oft is his gold complexion dimmed.
And every fair from fair sometimes declines,
By chance or nature's changing course untrimmed.
But thy eternal summer shall not fade,
Nor lose possession of the fair thou owest.
Nor shall death brag thou wandrest in his leafy shade
When in eternal lines to time thou growest,
So long as men can breathe or eyes can see,
So long lives this –

**File**  And this gives life –

**William**  Give life, live, give life –

**File**  And this gives life to thee.

*By the poem's end William, the File and Hugh sit in an embrace.*

**William**  Mother of God, who am I? Father in heaven, answer me. (*William sings.*) Dig the grave, dig the grave –

*The File sings.*

**File**
Bard meaning poet,
River meaning aibhne,
Bard meaning poet,
River meaning aibhne –

**William**  Aibhne, aibhne, aibh – aibh. Avon. Aibhne.

**File**  It is him.


**SCENE TWO**

*The forest. They sleep, apart from Annas and the File, who talk together. Annas is giving herbs to the File. The File has brought food.*

**Annas** These roots will guarantee forgetfulness, and these will ensure love. These leaves when crushed in liquid let the eyes see what they wish. These flowers if placed beneath a pillow break the bonds of man and wife. Take care with these frail stems. Their taste stops the human heart.

**File** They will be of use. Your food, hide it.

**Annas** File, I have something to tell you.

**File** Which is?

**Annas** I think I am loved by one of the slaves.

**File** You have hinted as much before.

**Annas** I know it now. I am kind to him. While the others sleep, I remove the cloth from his mouth. We have been talking of his strange life. File, have you heard of a place where people go and listen to stories?

**File** We tell our stories –

**Annas** But not in the way his people tell theirs. They pay to enter –

**File** Pay?

**Annas** Money. To enter. That is how they keep the theatre –

**File** Theatre?

**Annas** That is what they call this place, yes. In this theatre they can be kings or queens or men and women.

**File** These men are allowed to become women?

**Annas** They call it playing a woman. They can be in love or hate each other, kiss and kill each other, and not love nor die –

**File**  They can rise from the dead in this theatre?

**Annas**  It is a most extraordinary place. They can do and say and go anywhere in it.

**File**  The English have discovered this place?

**Annas**  It is a wonderful discovery.

**File**  I have heard it spoken of.

**Annas**  Who by? Where?

**File**  At the castle. This man, this stranger, William –

**Annas**  He is their companion. I think he must be their servant, and a lowly one at that. When Richard names him, he laughs. It did my heart good to hear him laughing in his distress.

**File**  That was kind of you, Annas. You must be kind always. It is your nature.

**Annas**  Am I loved by him?

**File**  You should be. And he is a man of good proportions, this Richard. You may even love him in return, but not too much! He is a captive.

**Annas**  I asked my father to untie each from the other, and my gentle king agreed. Now they may lie down and sleep. He even let me remove the cloths from their mouths at night. Am I wrong to let them speak to each other as we sleep?

**File**  No, that too is in your kind nature.

**Annas**  He makes me laugh.

**File**  How? Tell me.

**Annas**  His stories, they are so funny.

**File**  Stories about this theatre?

**Annas**  No, not really. He wants to leave that place. There he plays a king, and yet he is not. This troubles him, for he desires to be his own master. His is not the humblest heart. He wishes to be someone else.

**File**  What does he wish to be?

**Annas**  Richard would like to be a farmer.

**File**  How sweet.

**Annas**  Isn't it? He is so innocent. That is why he came to Ireland. He wished to obtain land.

**File**  Did he?

**Annas**  He heard about our prosperous province. He decided to come here and ask for land –

**File**  For he heard that when the English asked in Ireland, they did receive. Annas, you must promise me something.

**Annas**  What?

**File**  If you find an opportunity to take Richard's life, you must do that. Your royal parents keep them as their slaves. They are not so harmless as slaves. They are English. They are our enemy. They must be taken care of in the way that shall not harm us. You share your parents' royal blood. You have the right to remove any man who could further the cause of England in this country. That is a decree from God. Will you do that? Will you kill him?

**Annas**  How?

**File**  You must encourage him. Let him believe you are in love with him. Let him trust you. Let him think you are a weak woman. At the moment his trust is greatest, and you are at your weakest, then kiss him. Then, and only then, kiss him. It should be the kiss of death, frail as these stems, and he must not know it. But you must. Do you promise me that?

**Annas**  Yes, File.

**File**  I can trust you?

**Annas**  Yes.

**File**  Does he love you very much?

**Annas**  He begins to.

**File**  So his death may be difficult for you. Kill him, because he loves you and because he is English. He has no right to love you. It is the height of arrogance to love you. You must therefore take revenge. Sweet girl, it is the most fulfilling of all desires. Revenge, beautiful word. Say it.

**Annas**  Revenge.

**File**  For your father, the King.

**Annas**  For my father, the King.

**File**  For your mother, our Queen.

**Annas**  For my mother, our Queen.

**File**  Your country.

**Annas**  My country.

**File**  Your faith.

**Annas**  My faith.

**File**  By this new commandment, revenge, are you sworn to secrecy and to success.

**Annas**  I am so sworn.

**File**  Your vow never be broken.

**Annas**  Never.

**File**  Your heart never soften.

**Annas**  Never.

**File**  Your word be for eternity.

**Annas**  Eternity.

**File**  You are of our cause.

**Annas**  I am.

**File**  Go to sleep, child.

**Annas**  Sing to me, File.

*The File sings.*

**File**
When I was a child, a little child,
I did delight in rain and snow,
For rain and snow, they melt and go.
As I was a child, a little child.

And being a child, a little child,
I did believe in God and man,
But God and man, they upped and ran,
And left me with child, a little child.

Since I was with child, a little child,
I did protect in rain and snow,
Through rain and snow they forced me to go.
I am without child, a little child.
I am without child, am without child.

**Maeve**  You are instructing her well.

**File**  I am?

**Maeve**  Yes, as I desire.

**File**  Then I remain in my profession. To train the children
of our nobility in the art of living and the truths that go

beyond death. Once it was my task to instruct them as their File, to teach them law and language, the mastery of our metrics, the secrets of our poetry, the science of philosophy, the rules of our astronomy, the games of government, the divine power of courtesy – my heart is sore, remembering what once I was. A learned woman, wise to all knowledge; oh wise woman, oh File, so they would address me, most honoured in her society, most learned. Your young you gave me to reign with authority. Now I am reduced to this. Revenge. Did you hear what I told her?

**Maeve** You are instructing her well.

**File** I instruct her as is my duty.

**Maeve** To kill.

**File** Yes.

**Maeve** If she is her father's daughter, she will take revenge.

**File** Yes.

**Maeve** I think you are growing fond of our enemy, File. You have lived too long amongst them. They have changed you. Your heart is growing weak. Look at me, and remember what I was. I once knew silver plates and golden crown. The candles in my palace danced to greet me in their light. I bathed in warm water and my skin tasted silk. I would bathe in the blood of my enemies and wear their flesh for warmth before I would listen to their reasoning, but you, File, you have no stomach for blood.

**File** My Queen, I do as you bid.

**Maeve** A wise woman and a good servant, who knows her wisdom depends on her service to our authority. A servant, you are a servant, for all your wisdom. For all your intelligence, for all the praise and honour once bestowed on you, File, your power, your memories mean nothing, without the favour and desires of our authority. Remember that. We have ruled before Christ in this country. You were chosen to be our learned servant. To sing our glory. To praise our ancestors. To raise our children in that ancestral pride that they may sing their own glory. So you still take pride in that chosen position. Shall I make you even more proud? Your English master, Edmund, he is no different to you. He serves his queen as you served your king. He writes exalted verses to her as she sits in glory upon her throne. That is his dignity. You have no such dignity any more. You worship a king grown old before his time, foraging for sustenance in a forest, in danger of forgetting his own name. You are no longer his poet. You are his spy, as is Edmund the queen's spy. Do you think she, like us, values him for his vision? No, it is for his cunning. All wisdom comes down to this. And from our servant you have now truly turned into his, the Englishman's, and that is your cursed destiny.

**File** No, I am under no such curse. Do not put me under that curse.

**Maeve** Do not put yourself under it.

**File** My life, my lady, you are hard to me. How have I offended you so grievously to deserve such rebuke?

**Maeve** Recite my prayers, File.

**File** I shall not.

**Maeve** Why not?

**File** I am not worthy to speak your glory, great Queen.

**Maeve** My glory is past.

**File** Your glory is eternal as the sun.

**Maeve** The sun doth fade at night.

**File** Night shall not darken the greatness of your name.

**Maeve** My name shall be forgotten.

**File** It shall live for ever. Most valiant warrior, most true knight, most loyal in the faith of Christ, Maeve, queen of all, most loved, most loved, most loved.

**Maeve** My wise woman, my bard, most loved.

**File** My Queen.

**Maeve** What is happening at the castle?

**File** The stranger, William, is growing stronger.

**Maeve** Has his mind returned to reason?

**File** Nearly so.

**Maeve** And my son, Hugh?

**File** William may be in love with Hugh, I cannot tell if this will be of use to us.

**Maeve** I asked about Hugh.

**File** He grows in beauty.

**Maeve** And in strength?

**File** Yes, in strength.

**Maeve** He will not betray us.

**File** No.

**Maeve** You are sure of this?

**File** Dear Queen, he is your son as surely as I am your servant. Why do you doubt us?

**Maeve** I did doubt you at first, when this plan to defeat the English from within their walls was put to me. I knew the hatred that had grown between you and my son. So dangerous an undertaking required love and trust on both your parts. Do you still love him?

**File** That is lost.

**Maeve** Trust him?

**File** I have to.

**Maeve** And he you. I am weary, File. I have lived too long.

**Sweney** Maeve?

**Maeve** My lord?

**Sweney** What has become of my kingdom? I do not remember.

**Maeve** It is lost. We must try to get it back, my king.

**Sweney** Christ alone is king, some say. Had they adorned Christ with feathers he would have flown above the Cross, but instead they chose a crown of thorns and in revenge, this crown he has handed on to all other kings. It is a blessing to be relieved of the crown that is carved from thorn. I pricked my finger on my father's head and so I became king. King. I shall walk down among the people, my subjects. Maeve, walk with me.

*They walk together.*

Are my people happy to be my subjects, dear wife?

**Maeve** There are rumours of discontent.

**Sweney** I have failed them in some way, have I?

**Maeve** They have failed you, my husband.

**Sweney** They would not defend me?

**Maeve** Yes, to the death, my love, but they themselves are nearly all dead, your subjects.

**Sweney**  There were so many. How have they all died?

**Maeve**  Starvation.

**Sweney**  Starvation. And I survived? How?

**Maeve**  You went mad, my dear husband. That is how.

**Sweney**  Am I still mad?

**Maeve**  Yes.

**Sweney**  And you?

**Maeve**  Yes.

**Sweney**  Where do you hear the rumours of discontent?

**Maeve**  In the murmurs of the forest. They crowd in upon me. They fall from the leaves, they rise from the earth.

**Sweney**  We have fallen to earth, my goddess. You are my Athena, my Aphrodite, my Hero. Olympus is bare tonight. They have stolen the sun, our enemies. Dionysius sleeps for ever, I fear. No solemn acts of worship attend us now. Our fate is sealed till death. We are no longer divine beings, far above the destiny of mere mortals.

**File**  My lord, we are mortal.

**Sweney**  We die?

**File**  We die.

**Sweney**  Change and chance have befallen us. This mutable earth is now our lot. Brother earth, greetings from your mad king. We race, we rant, we dwell in darkness, until we dim to death. Is the lord listening? Is he in heaven or is he in hell? Oh god of change and chance, revenge me.

**File**  You shall be revenged.

**Sweney**  Perhaps we should sleep. In our dreams we may be ourselves again.

34

**Maeve** Aye, my love, in sleep a king.

**File** A man will come amongst us. He will be from a river. The water shall save him. The river shall reveal him. He shall speak our stories.

**Sweney** Goodnight, goodnight.

**Maeve** Goodnight.

*Sweney lies down to sleep.*

You are dismissed, File.

**File** My homage to my lord and lady.

**Maeve** It is accepted.

*The File leaves. Maeve lies beside Sweney. Silence.*

**Ben** Jesus, Richard I'm frightened.

**Richard** They'll hear you, they'll cut our tongues out.

**Ben** If I'm reading this story right, the king, so-called, has lost his kingdom and his mind, and the good lady wife's gone off her rocker to keep him company. The daughter, who fancies you, is a nympho –

**Richard** How is she a nympho?

**Ben** Because she fancies you. The File moves between two camps, ours, and this one. She's up to badness. But in all this, Richard lad, ours is not to reason why, ours is not to ask. To keep our heads it is best to lie low, don't ask and don't look. Humour them. In the land of the mad, go mad, old son. And in this bloody country, there are only the mad.

**Richard** You're half-mad already, do you know that? What am I saying, half-mad? Completely mad. You said come to Ireland in the first place, you really wanted to come. How could I have believed such claptrap as you and him were spouting. Ireland's opening up, you said, and there's no theatre over there. It'll be a novelty, a first, you said, we'll clean up. A bit of money for the taking, and land there, you said, it's going a-begging. They're handing it out to anyone who wants it. You just have to be English, that's all. I believed you, so I went. You knew I'd believe you. I always wanted my own patch of land. You knew that. So I blame you for all of this.

**Ben**  That's not fair. William thought of it first.

**Richard**  William thought of it first? William has never had a thought in his head. The only reason he's been let stay with us is because he can write down what we say. He learned to write, he went to school, we didn't, and he's still more stupid than us put together.

**Ben**  Come on, you're being hard. He's strung together a fair few plots and he does know how to polish up a speech.

**Richard**  Oh does he? I'm glad you think so. He doesn't. He doesn't think he writes his own plays. Don't you remember?

**Ben**  Oh yes, the cats.

**Richard**  Yes, the cats. I can't write without a cat in the building, he says. We had cats pouring over the place, because William needed to write. Hello, William, that's a good piece of writing. Don't thank me, he says. It's the cats. They communicate a feline energy, a leonine power, they're my inspiration. What kind of man thinks a cat writes his plays?

**Ben**  He believes they're in touch with a superior power of the universe and show a brilliant understanding of the human mind. I think it's his way of landing women. They like men who like cats.

**Richard**  He's mad. And he's molly.

**Ben**  No, he's not.

**Richard**  He's molly, he's into men.

**Ben**  How do you know?

**Richard**  I've had him. Once.

**Ben**  What was he like?

**Richard**  He meowed.

**Ben**  That's perverted.

**Richard**  Go to sleep, Ben.

  *Silence.*

**Ben**  If he's alive, he might still save us.

**Richard**  He might.

**Ben**  I hope we get out of this alive.

**Richard**  Yes. (*Silence.*) We've never been in a worse spot, have we?

**Ben**  Obviously you've never played in the Wakefield Mystery Cycle.

**Richard**  Goodnight.

**Ben**  Goodnight, Richard.

  *They sleep. Niall and Donal enter, armed.*

**Donal**  They have grown ragged, our followers.

**Niall**  You judge them by their attire?

**Donal**  Yes, as they judge themselves.

**Niall**  They are still men and women.

**Donal**  Scarcely so. I wish we could be as we were.

**Niall** Younger?

**Donal** Yes. Do you miss your brother?

**Niall** He has his duty to do.

**Donal** And you have your sister. (*Silence.*) You once wished to be a priest.

**Niall** To follow in your footsteps. I have stopped so wishing.

**Donal** I have lost you.

**Niall** You have lost me.

**Donal** Our holy father in Rome –

**Niall** Is our holy father in Rome?

**Donal** You are committing sin. Your sister commits sin.

**Niall** Our followers are few, but they are gathering. When I give the word, they will commit sin against our enemies for the evil done against them, and then all sins will be forgiven.

**Donal** I shall rest beside your father and your mother.

**Niall** Do so, good confessor.

**Donal** You no longer believe in me.

**Niall** I no longer do.

**Donal** Jesus is merciful.

**Niall** His mother is kind.

**Donal** Respect the Virgin. Defile the Virgin and we are lost.

*He lies beside the king and queen. Niall lies beside Annas, his arms around her. She curls around him. Richard sees their embrace.*

## SCENE THREE

*Early in the morning in both the forest and the castle. Elizabeth sits nursing a child. There is the rising sun both in the castle and the forest. Annas sits looking at Richard. The File enters with a jug of milk.*

**File**  Good lady, you have not slept.

**Annas**  Do you like this hour of morning?

**File**  The milk is warm. Please drink.

**Annas**  Are there mornings as soft as these in England?

*The File lifts the jug to Elizabeth's mouth. Elizabeth drinks the milk and then spits it at the File.*

I will not let them harm you.

**File**  Are you afraid I would kill you. See, I won't.

*The File drinks some of the milk.*

**Annas**  You're crying. Your face is full of tears. (*She touches Richard's face.*) You think I have betrayed you. With my own brother. Poor man. You have little faith in me.

**File**  Our master needs you to keep your strength. He has told you so. Good lady Elizabeth, you are wife to Edmund. Gentle lady, let me help you. I ask only to serve you.

*Elizabeth weeps. Music.*

**Annas**  When I was a child, a girl, I used to weep in the morning, if I could not sleep. Our wise woman, the File, she would nurse me on her knee.

*Elizabeth kisses the child as it sleeps. She sings in harmony with Annas's speech.*

**Elizabeth**
  Little child, little child,
  Mother mild, mother mild,
  Little child, little child,
  Mother mild, mother mild.

**Annas**  The File told me my tears were from God. He was creating the earth and wept for its beauty. It was but a dream, this beauty. Do not weep for it.

  *Elizabeth continues to sing as Annas speaks.*

**Elizabeth**
  Child so sweet, child of mine,
  You will learn the world in time,
  Child so sweet, child of mine,
  You will learn the world in time.

**Annas**  Do not weep for the world's beauty. It is like weeping for Eden. And Eden is but a dream, a paradise. Soon it will disappear, she said, Eden, paradise, as I would disappear some day soon.

  *The music ceases.*

I was weeping for my own death. Why do you weep?

  *Silence.*

**File**  Lady Elizabeth, when I lost all in these late wars of Munster, I too was afraid to sleep. I could not close my eyes, as you cannot. I know you cannot sleep. To lose my senses in sleep would be to lose all, for all I had left was life itself, and I do love my life. I love my home that I had lost.

**Elizabeth**  I long for my home.

**File**  For England?

**Richard**  England.

**Elizabeth** (*sings*)
> Come sweet April, I will dress in yellow,
> And like the primrose, bedeck the meadow,
> I will dare the wind to dance through the trees
> And pay good heed to my mother's loud pleas,
> Come live with me in England, in England,
> Come live with me in England, sweet England.

**Richard** (*sings*)
> Come soft July I will dress in red,
> And like the rosebud, scented the bed,
> I will tell the sun to shower its hues,
> And pay good heed to my father's sweet rues.
> Come love with me in England, in England,
> Come love with me in England, soft England.

*Elizabeth and Richard sing in chorus.*

**Chorus**
> Come cold winter, I will dress in black,
> And like the raven caw the air to crack,
> I will fill the moon till it's full to burst
> With my salty tears, now my days are cursed,
> When I remember England, sweet England,
> Now I remember England, soft England,
> For I have lived in England, sweet England,
> And I would love in England, soft England.

*The File gives the milk to Elizabeth and she drinks. Richard tries to kiss Annas but she gently refuses. The File takes the jug from Elizabeth. Annas replaces the gag around Richard's mouth. Elizabeth nods to the child and asks for the milk, but the File drinks it. Richard holds out his arms to Annas, but she rejects them.*

**Annas** Your voice is that of a good man.

**File** How beautifully you sing.

**Annas**  How sorely you miss your home.

**File**  You love England dearly. Could you come to love this country also?

**Annas**  Had you known Ireland in a happier time, you would not pine so for England. Ireland has changed as we have changed. As we must change.

*Light fades on the forest.*

**Elizabeth**  I long for my home.

**File**  For England?

**Elizabeth**  England.

**File**  Our master Edmund truly loves this landscape. Its rivers and forests, its shores and haunted places. He asks us their names. We tell him. It is for his poem in praise of our queen. When we speak these names to Edmund, he hears through our voices why they are haunted, for they are bereft of our people now. It has become your land. Love it.

**Elizabeth**  It is not my land, and it will never be, and were it mine of what worth would my love be to Ireland?

**File**  That same love may be of worth to your own life. It may even bring you back to England. I have said how your husband finds this land to his attraction. My lady, you know the contrariness of men, their weak minds do not stay steadfast in their desires, and they do hate a rival for their affections.

*Elizabeth laughs.*

**Elizabeth**  You fondly imagine I could come to love you, a servant, a washerwoman –

**File**  My lady mishears. I advise you to change your affections. Turn your hatred of Ireland to love of it, then it may be your husband's love will turn to hatred.

**Elizabeth**  That is the thinking of a fool.

**File**  A fool? Perhaps I am. But it is thinking which pays homage to the principle of change, and change controls this earth and all its workings. I am proof. Once no man nor woman would dare call me fool. I once had servants, washerwomen, I too have suffered change in these late wars of Munster –

**Elizabeth**  Damn these late wars of Munster –

**File**  Indeed, for these same wars do contradict my argument. The English won, the Irish lost. There is no change to that pattern. But having won us, come to love us. Change your hate to love.

*Elizabeth leaves. The File sings.*

**File**
    The gods possess a power strange,
    For all things turn to dust and change,
    Mankind, the sky, the rivered sea
    Sing of mutabilitie.

    Ladies fair and men of valour
    Flower a day and then do wither.
    Mankind, the sky, the rivered sea
    Sing of mutabilitie.

    I call on Death, most trusted friend,
    To bring your exile to its end,
    Mankind, the sky, the rivered sea
    Sing of mutabilitie.

    The gods possess a power strange,
    For all things turn to dust and change,
    Mankind, the sky, the rivered sea
    Sing of mutabilitie.

# Act Three

## SCENE ONE

*Edmund, Elizabeth, their children, William, Hugh and the File assemble for prayer.*

**Edmund**  Dear Lord, there was never anything by the wit of man so well devised, or so sure established, which in continuance of time has not been corrupted: as, among other things, it may plainly appear in the Common Prayer in the Church, commonly called Divine Service. As we exult thee, oh Lord, for the gifts of the earth, so do we praise thee for the faith you have reformed in us, and for the love of heaven, for the sake of sweet salvation, we sing to you hosanna, in this song of common prayer.

*They sing 'The Song of Common Prayer' in chorus.*

**Chorus**
There is no God but God alone.
To speak his name is holy sound.
Our souls that mesh with blood and bone,
Do clothe the grace that we have found.
Great King of Heaven, open wide
The gates to thy good bower of bliss
And guide thy subjects by thy side
In fortitude and righteousness.

He sweetly scented my frail soul,
I hand that posy to my lord,
And in return he did reveal
The truth of his unending word.
Great King of Heaven, father dear,
Your brood you house and feed and bathe.
This song we sing of common prayer

44

Decrees we stand in your own faith.

**Edmund**  There is no God but God alone.

**Chorus**  Amen.

*They sit for breakfast, the File and Hugh serving.*

**William**  This country of Ireland that you have now lived in and know is by repute a goodly and commodious soil. I wonder why no course is taken to turn it to good use and to turn that nation to better government and civility.

**Edmund**  Wise counsels have already been cast about reformation of this realm of Ireland.

**William**  And these reformations have not succeeded in Ireland.

**Edmund**  It may be Almighty God has not appointed the time for her reformation. It may be he keeps this land in this unquiet state still for some secret scourge and this scourge may come to England through Ireland. It's hard to know, and it leaves much to fear, for the Irish do persist in their evils.

**William**  Which particular evils?

**Edmund**  Ancient, long grown evils. Errors of law, custom, religion.

**William**  Law? The Irish have laws?

**Edmund**  These laws are repugnant to God's law, and to man's. Murder can be forgiven through the mercy of money paid to the child or the wife of the murdered man. Through this vile law many murderers live quite freely amongst them. All quite concealed.

**William**  A most wicked law indeed.

**Edmund**  Quite concealed. They are quite concealed.

**William**  Their customs?

**Edmund**  They are steeped in courage. They are very
valiant and hardy. For the most part they have great
endurance of cold, work and hunger. They are strong of
hand, swift of foot, vigilant. They are ever present in the
greatest peril, for they scorn death greatly.

**William**  Are you saying by this that the Irishman is a very
brave soldier?

**Edmund**  Yes, in a rudimentary kind of service. But they
have not served abroad and the simplest weapon is a mystery to their intelligence.

**William**  Do they value courage above all intelligence?

**Edmund**  No, they value cunning. There is also among the
Irish a certain kind of Bards who are – who are poets.

**William**  Poets?

**Edmund**  A certain kind, I say. These Bards are held in
high regard amongst the Irish. Their verses receive great
reward and reputation.

**William**  You surely would not quarrel with such prac-
tices?

**Edmund**  There are poets who labour in their writings to
better the manners of men. Irish Bards are of another
mind. The most licentious, bold and lawless men, the
most dangerous and most desperate, these are the men
they set up and glorify in all parts of disobedience and
rebellious disposition, these they praise to the people and
make an example for the young to follow. In all this their
Bards lead the way, indulging their direst fantasies.

*Elizabeth rises from the table.*

**Elizabeth**  My husband, do you detect in your words any

sign of yourself? These Irish poets praise their betters to line their pockets, as you do, Edmund. You can conjure any sour vice into sweet virtue through honeyed words, as do they. And these Bards should praise a most beautiful and sweet country as any is under heaven. There are many goodly rivers, replenished most abundantly with all sorts of fish. These rivers are sprinkled with very many sweet islands, and lakes, like little seas, carry even ships upon their waters. There are good ports and havens that open upon England, as if they invite us to come to them, and so we have come, to be lords of all the seas, of all the world of Ireland.

**Edmund**  Lord, how quickly can this country alter our nature.

**Elizabeth**  I have come to love this country as surely as my husband has come to learn this country through those we have saved from their country. Dear servants, come forward.

*The File and Hugh do so, their heads bowed.*

From these kind servants he has gathered much more knowledge of those Irish laws and customs than he has elaborated for you. From these servants also I have learned to love this land. In my mind I turned this country into a nest of thieves, finding in it only that which is infected to be Irish-like. I admit my error as Edmund admits so readily to their errors of law and custom. But in them, I can trace the roots of reformation and revelation. Yes, I have saved them, but they too have saved me.

*The File and Hugh kneel before Elizabeth. They take her hand and kiss it. She touches their heads.*

**Edmund**  Rise.

*They do so.*

Sit, Elizabeth.

*She does so.*

The third error is of religion. They need ministers of our
faith who are their own countrymen. They send their
young men to university beyond the seas. To Reims,
Douai and Louvain. They then return and lurk secretly in
their houses and in corners of the country. They do hurt
and hindrance to the true religion. The sick body of this
land sickens its mind and soul in allegiance to heathen,
superstitious Rome. Their hearts they still give to Rome.
Out of the abundance of the heart, the tongue speaks, and
here it speaks of Rome and of saint and of virgin and
statue and relic and monk and blasphemies against our
sweet Saviour. Such blasphemy must be cut from the
tongue. Such beliefs must be destroyed. It is for the good
of the heathen people. They must not be left to lament in
the devil's darkness, and they do lament immeasurably,
lamenting their dead. Their ceaseless cries through the late
wars of Munster haunt me. It is as if they have no faith
nor hope of salvation. For charity's sake, I shall give them
faith and hope. I shall lead them to salvation.

*Silence. A child sings.*

**Child**
> You sweetly scented my frail soul,
> I gave that posy to my lord,
> And in return he did reveal
> The truth of his unending word.

*Edmund sings lowly.*

**Edmund**
> Great King of Heaven, open wide
> The gates to thy good bower of bliss,

48

And guide thy subjects by thy side
In fortitude and righteousness.

*Silence.*

**Hugh** God bless the work.

**Edmund** Yes. God bless the work. Be about your business.

*Hugh and the File exit.*

My wife.

*Edmund and William stand and bow to Elizabeth. She does likewise and exits with the children.*

**William** Dear friend, I have not thanked you adequately for the kindness you displayed to me through my sickness and stay in your home. It is beyond Christian charity.

**Edmund** Nothing is beyond Christian charity.

**William** Indeed, nothing is.

**Edmund** For an intelligent man, you speak in such a predictable manner. Is this a fashion now in London? Predictability?

**William** Why do you think I'm intelligent?

*Silence.*

**Edmund** I have stopped writing.

**William** No gentler shepherd may be found –

**Edmund** The last time I was in London, the queen looked at me. How is the queen?

**William** Soldiering on.

*Silence.*

**Edmund** She will never marry, you know. She will die a

virgin. If she were to marry, it should be to an Irishman. Were she to marry him and conceive a peace between us, there would be gentleness in the house at night.

*Silence.*

**William**  Gentle spirit, from whose pen large streams of honey and sweet nectar flow –

**Edmund**  William, some nights I think I am our sovereign. Am I going mad? I have stopped writing.

**William**  You are too much alone in this place.

**Edmund**  I am not alone in this place. You are here. Why are you here?

**William**  Gentle shepherd, I have long learned from your poetry. I beat time to its music, I submit myself to its virtue. I have so deeply aspired to your exalted heights of invention, and in my work – do you know my work?

**Edmund**  No.

**William**  I am a playwright. (*Silence.*) I write plays.

**Edmund**  I surmised. Why are you here?

**William**  It is difficult to ask it.

**Edmund**  Ask it. (*Silence.*) Ask it.

**William**  I'd like to leave the theatre and get a job in the civil service.

**Edmund**  When I was last in London, I understood the theatre was now the civil service.

**William**  Times have changed. The fashion is now subversive.

**Edmund**  The fashion will change. Stay in the theatre.

**William**  It no longer needs me.

**Edmund**  As my poem no longer needs me. It has out-stripped my powers.

**William**  Your powers are very great.

**Edmund**  As my nation is great. What is my nation?

**William**  England.

**Edmund**  England no longer needs me. I am abandoned here in exile.

**William**  You are recognized as a secretary of the crown.

**Edmund**  A poor servant of the crown. Poverty is my reward and my reputation. Is it yours, William?

**William**  My family were prominent in the county of Warwickshire.

**Edmund**  Were? There were many Catholics in Warwickshire. They lost prominence. (*Silence.*) You are a Catholic? You were a Catholic?

**William**  I am troubled.

**Edmund**  I am not. (*Silence.*) There is no God but God alone, and we are his servants.

**William**  And God alone guided me in fortitude and right-eousness to this castle. You alone, great poet –

**Edmund**  I have ceased to write –

**William**  Great poet –

**Edmund**  The poem, the great poem is unfinished –

**William**  Great poet, if I enter the service of the queen, I will devote my life to her glory, to her empire. Your wife spoke of the lords of the sea, the lords of the world, this is what we are, lords, lords –

**Edmund**  We are the English in Ireland –

**William** We have started to conquer, we have conquered –

**Edmund** We have started to go mad.

**William** Let me assist you in the continuation of that conquest.

**Edmund** What shall you give me in return?

**William** I am poor.

**Edmund** As am I. Poor poet, poor William –

**William** Why did you think I was intelligent? (*Silence.*) I do not know if I am intelligent. (*Silence.*) I know how to lie intelligently, to lie beautifully. I have taken this knowledge and placed it on a stage. I have written in the vernacular so that all who see and hear must first understand and afterwards embrace the doctrine of my plays, and thereby be led, knowingly, to what salvation is contained therein. I have paraded before the people those thoughts, those images, those words, those hearts, those minds, that until the time of reformation lay concealed in the corrupt cloisters and confined courts of kings – let those see who would see, hear who would hear. I let the lives I create burn in brilliant, everlasting fire. I have been in the business of discovering fire. And I have burned myself to ashes in the pursuit of fire. (*Silence.*) I repeat my thanks to you. God has sent me to be saved in this place. I come to this country to plead my case before you. I leave myself to your charity.

*Silence.*

**Edmund** I shall consider your application. Good day.

**William** Good day, gentle poet.

*Edmund exits. The File moves from the shadows, where she has been listening.*

**File**  Good sir, I have a gift for you.

**William**  A gift?

*She gives him a yellow flower.*

Beautiful.

**File**  Most delicate and graceful stem.

**William**  Graceful, yes.

**File**  A flower for Our Lady's Day. Your devotion to the Virgin Mary is great. You called to her without cease in your illness. I nursed you when you were fevered. You spoke of Our Lady as one who believes in her.

**William**  In my fever. Did I call or did I whisper?

**File**  Her name? In whispers.

**William**  Who heard me whisper so?

**File**  Myself, and Hugh.

**William**  Only the servants?

**File**  Only the servants.

**William**  You must not breathe such knowledge to anyone, good woman. It is blasphemy.

**File**  Blasphemy? To believe in the Virgin?

**William**  Blasphemy to worship her.

**File**  Unless she is an Englishwoman.

**William**  That is treason.

**File**  That is ambition, for the path to greatness leads to Elizabeth, virgin queen of England. Is this the path you follow to Protestant greatness, William?

**William**  In the name of Mary, will you betray me?

**File**  How deeply do you believe?

**William**  On Our Lady's Day my mother cast daisies into the River Avon in secret homage to the queen of heaven, so many frail stems I thought the river pied with the flowers of worship. And as I was a child, and did love my mother, so I did love the mother of Christ.

**File**  In the name of Christ you will not be betrayed.

**William**  Then do not speak to me of these secrets, for it is death to all ambition to believe such.

**File**  I do not wish for your death, nor would I cry halt to your ambition. I would wash that ambition free from sin in the waters of this same Avon and present it as your gift to Christ and his mother, were I the mother you loved. I have longed to speak to you. I have been waiting to speak to you. My people have been waiting.

**William**  I know neither you nor your people.

*Light on Maeve and Sweney, in each other's arms, watched by Donal.*
   *Light on Hugh, watching the File and William.*

**Sweney**  Who am I? I have forgotten.

**Maeve**  You are my husband.

**File**  We have a language we are losing. Maybe it is already lost.

**Sweney**  Am I not your father?

**Maeve**  You are father to your subjects, and I am your subject, dear King, dear husband.

**File**  In that language you are a poet and would be called a Bard, and you come from the river which in that language is the Avon.

**Sweney**  Am I king of the earth, its rivers and seas?

**File**  A Bard of Avon. A poet from the river.

**Sweney**  If I am so, I command the waters to drown me.

**File**  Good William, the riddle is solved. A man shall come from the river, he shall speak our stories, he shall sing the song of songs.

**Sweney**  Will you die with me?

**Maeve**  I will.

**File**  The riddle is solved.

**William**  What riddle?

**File**  The riddle of who you are.

> *Light on Annas, Niall, Ben and Richard. Annas releases herself from Niall and goes to Richard. Niall watches them.*

**William**  Bard of Avon? What an extraordinary description. Quite barbaric really. I don't like it.

**Annas**  Do you have a wife in England?

**Richard**  Yes.

**William**  I'm not as your poets are. I don't praise disobedience and I don't spread discontent.

**File**  No, you are discontent yourself.

**Annas**  Does she play with you in this theatre?

> *Richard laughs.*

**Ben**  Ladies don't, dear – play.

**File**  I heard you talking, I listened, I saw by the light of your fire.

**Annas** If I were to go with you to England, would you leave her?

**File** You believe it's dead, that fire, but it can still burn.

**Maeve** My lord, we must live.

**Annas** I want to go with you to England.

**File** Why do you now begin to fear it? Have you begun to lose faith in fire?

**Annas** I can give you safe passage to the sea.

**File** You wish to turn away from the all-consuming theatre, why?

**Sweney** I am tired.

**File** I have imagined this place.

**Sweney** I wish to die.

**File** Is it not now a sacred dwelling? Is it not a temple where the remembered dead rise from their graves?

**Sweney** I have seen too many dead.

**File** Sins are forgiven there.

**Sweney** They died for my sins.

**File** Cries are heard.

**Sweney** I pray to God for forgiveness.

**File** Prayers are answered.

**Sweney** He is tired too and no longer listens.

**Annas** I can get you to England, do you hear me? Speak to me.

**File** Is it not there that your race now speaks to God? Is that theatre not your country's true place of reformation?

**Ben**  Richard, answer her.

**File**  Are you not a priest in this new religion that may attach itself most secretly, most devoutly to the old abandoned faith?

**Annas**  I will leave my mother and father.

**File**  Your father's, your mother's faith.

**Richard**  And go where?

**File**  You are a Catholic in honest service to a Protestant nation that shall keep the true faith through your fire, your theatre. It is a holy place of great, good magic –

**William**  These theatres are rough.

**File**  The grace of god is rough.

**Richard**  I don't have a wife – I have a whore.

**Maeve**  My gentle husband –

**Sweney**  Too gentle – censure me for that.

**Annas**  What is a whore?

**File**  Through that rough grace you have come to me to be saved for Ireland, for England.

**Ben**  Me, when I was younger.

**Richard**  And me.

**Maeve**  I will never censure you for that gentleness.

**File**  William, solve the riddle yourself.

**Richard**  We'd sell our arses for a plate of bacon.

**Ben**  A plate, not a slice.

**File**  Tell our story, our suffering to the people of England.

**Richard**  And so will you in England.

**File**  That is the answer.

**Richard**  An Irish whore, her soft face growing hard.

**Maeve**  I am warrior enough for both of us.

**File**  Through you there will be peace between these nations.

**Richard**  I will sell you rather than let me starve.

**File**  The war between us will end.

*Light on Edmund and Elizabeth.*

The war must end.

**Edmund**  How have you come to love Ireland?

**File**  It is tearing the souls of us both to ribbons.

**Richard**  You'll whore for me in the theatre.

**File**  William, we have fought for centuries.

**Edmund**  Does this new love exclude me from your heart?

**File**  We approach the end of this century.

**Edmund**  Do you do this to defy me?

**File**  Let it be an end to war.

**Edmund**  Answer me, Elizabeth.

**Richard**  So will you still save us?

**File**  Or must it continue for another hundred years?

**Maeve**  I will fight with all my heart and blood.

**File**  And another hundred years?

**Annas**  I will do as you ask me to do in England.

**File**  And another hundred years?

**Elizabeth**  Yes, I do it to defy you.

**File**  And another hundred years?

**William**  I do not wish to understand you.

**Elizabeth**  Will you please me and leave Ireland?

**File**  You are not well pleased with my passion.

**Richard**  You would leave your most loving brother?

**File**  I shall give you what pleases you.

**Sweney**  I am afraid of death, Maeve.

**File**  Hugh pleases you. Have him.

**Richard**  Will you leave your brother?

**Edmund**  I cannot leave Ireland.

**File**  He is my gift to you, as the theatre is God's gift to a Catholic who must speak in the language of a Protestant.

**Maeve**  I do not fear death, my lord.

**Edmund**  You cannot leave without me.

**Annas**  He is only my brother.

**File**  Take Hugh – love him.

**William**  You speak of a sin fit only for the flames.

**File**  A flame you long to warm your flesh against, a flame you worship.

**Elizabeth**  Then as you desire, I'll die beside you.

**Maeve**  We must live to fight.

**William**  Tempt me not.

**File**  You tempt yourself.

**Richard**  Lie with me, whore.

*He pulls her towards him.*

**Ben** Don't mind me, I'm the Great Bed of Ware.

*She resists.*

**Annas** They'll kill you if we're caught.

**File** Take him.

**William** He does not want me.

**File** He may.

**Annas** I will lie with you in England.

**Edmund** Are you still my wife?

**File** He is my gift. Now give me yours.

**Ben** Will you get us back home?

**Elizabeth** I have always been your wife.

**File** Your gift that I may tell our story on the stage.

**William** There is no gift.

**Edmund** Will you consent to sleep with me tonight?

**William** That is only your dream. You will wake from it. As I have.

**Elizabeth** I will consent to die with you tonight.

**File** When I die, I will waken and find it was not a dream.

**Hugh** File.

**Edmund** Elizabeth.

**William** It is a way of dying, yes.

**Annas** I would die for you.

**William** This dream, this theatre.

**Richard**  I would not for you.

**Niall**  Annas.

**Elizabeth**  We will die in Ireland.

**File**  But the dead have risen before.

**Maeve**  We must avenge our dead.

**File**  The dead will rise again.

**Donal**  My lord, my lady, vengeance.

**Maeve**  We will see the English dead.

**Edmund**  I will not die in Ireland.

**File**  In this your theatre you will make our dead rise, William. You will raise our Irish dead, Englishman.

# Act Four

*The forest.*

**Ben**  Why do you think it's so quiet?

**Richard**  They must have gone hunting.

**Ben**  Now's the time she might let us go.

**Richard**  Yes, she might.

**Ben**  Richard, you won't leave me here? You'll take me with you? I am so frightened.

**Richard**  Don't be.

**Ben**  I still think they might kill us.

**Richard**  They won't, love.

**Ben**  You still love me?

**Richard**  With all my heart I do.

**Ben**  Are you sure?

**Richard**  Yes.

**Ben**  So you won't leave me?

**Richard**  No.

**Ben**  You're a good man, Richard. People are good. One good thing about the Irish – have you heard them say a bad word against the Jews?

**Richard**  You're not Jewish, Ben.

**Ben**  I have played Jewish. Very successfully. So there were rumours, of course. I've played French and Italian as well. No rumours there. I've never played Welsh – there are limits.

**Richard** Remember the Welsh bit William brought among us?

**Ben** Speak to me in your language, sing to me in your language.

**Richard** He even wrote him a part in Welsh because he wouldn't learn English.

**Ben** He couldn't – his medical condition.

**Richard** A hole in his ear.

**Ben** A hole in his arse and William was often up it.

**Richard** That's not the story he tells in Welsh.

**Ben** You mean –

**Richard** What do you think?

**Ben** Well, Owen Glendower, you could knock me down with a leek.

**Richard** The Welsh bit got his week's wages out of William.

**Ben** He was worth the week's wages.

**Richard** He was, Ben.

**Ben** Whatever happened to him?

**Richard** He married the Earl of Southampton. I was Juno at the wedding Masque.

**Ben** I wasn't invited.

**Richard** You were playing Jewish at the time.

**Ben** Thank you.

*The beginnings of a storm.*

**Richard** We're going to live, Ben. We're going to get back home.

**Ben** Yes, Richard, we are.

### SCENE TWO

*The castle. They sit almost huddled together.*

**Edmund** It is for the best that tonight we stay close beside each other. Our enemy is at ease with the wildness of the elements. It is now that they may strike. I will watch the castle. William, Hugh, stay within the sound of my wife and children. File, sleep near my family.

*The men and women, with the children, separate into sleeping quarters. Edmund speaks to himself.*

The very wind and rain become the worst rebels in all Ireland, turning treacherously against me, against my sovereign and my Saviour. Lord in heaven, must the defender of your faith tremble in fear and panic at the terrible prospect of this exile? My Faerie Queen, most holy, most temperate, most chaste, most loyal, most just, most courteous majesty, hear my humble petition, Elizabeth of England. I am looking that I may leave Ireland, and if that not be granted to me, then give me leave to die, but I would fain die in England. The very soil of this corrupt land does corrupt my brain, and my sick imaginings devour my sense and reason. I fear to sleep, for in sleep my father rises from his grave to comfort his heartsore dreaming son. This night the gusts of grief do tear this same heart to pieces. Elizabeth, by my words shall you be known to all men. By your mercy shall you be known to me. Hear me, Elizabeth. (*Silence.*) Elizabeth?

64

*Silence. Fade on Edmund. Light on the File and Elizabeth, who sit sewing.*

**File** You will not answer the master? (*Silence.*) Will I see what troubles him?

**Elizabeth** You will sit and do your work with me.

**File** As you wish.

**Elizabeth** As I command.

**File** Your wish is my command.

**Elizabeth** If I told you to bark, would you bark?

**File** I believe in certain quarters our voices are referred to as the growling of a dog, so if you asked me to bark, I would speak and satisfy your demand.

**Elizabeth** Where did you hear that your voices resembled the growling of a dog?

*The File growls lowly. Elizabeth laughs. The File suddenly goes on all fours and growls. Elizabeth claps her hands. The File crawls towards Elizabeth. Elizabeth whistles. The File licks Elizabeth's hand. Elizabeth pats the File's hand. The File bites Elizabeth's hand. Elizabeth grabs the File's hand and bites back.*

That is the way I tame wild animals.

**File** Is it the way you tame wild thoughts?

**Elizabeth** I do not entertain wild thoughts.

**File** Not even about your husband.

**Elizabeth** My husband? Wild thoughts? (*She laughs.*) We met on the day of midsummer. I charmed his heart to mine. The spell I cast bewitched him. We wedded and made merry. And so we did besport ourselves to Time's most tempting music that wearies the staunchest love and wears out the bravest limbs. Our limbs entwined – our limbs entwine like lovers, still, but only like lovers. (*Silence.*) The night we married, we did conceive.

**File**  I have conceived also.

**Elizabeth**  And your child?

**File**  Lost.

**Elizabeth**  Dead? (*Silence.*) How do your people respond to death?

**File**  They laugh at it. It is a habit amongst us, a custom, to laugh when we should cry.

**Elizabeth**  You are a mad race.

**File**  If you say so.

**Elizabeth**  You'd put your hand into the fire if it were to defy the English.

**File**  No. The fire burns. Are you afraid of fire?

**Elizabeth**  Should I not be?

**File**  I do not know.

**Elizabeth**  If I asked you to prick your finger, would you?

**File**  Give me your hand.

*Elizabeth does so. The File winds thread about Elizabeth's finger. She bends and bites the thread.*

Elizabeth.

*Fade on the File and Elizabeth. Light on William and Hugh. Already half-drunk, they share a jug of wine. William belches.*

**William**  Forgive me.

**Hugh**  Forgiven.

66

**William**  Forgiven. Spoken like a gentleman. Like an Irishman. You have beautiful manners.

**Hugh**  Beautiful.

*Silence.*

**William**  Do you love your master?

**Hugh**  Yes.

**William**  Why do you love him?

**Hugh**  Manners.

**William**  Beautiful.

**Hugh**  To beauty. (*Hugh drinks.*)

**William**  To beauty. (*William drinks.*) Do you love that woman? Fool or File, whatever she's called.

**Hugh**  She is no fool.

**William**  You defend her, you love her.

**Hugh**  I did love her.

**William**  Did you marry her?

**Hugh**  No.

**William**  Do you marry? Do the Irish marry?

**Hugh**  We do.

**William**  I did.

**Hugh**  I know.

**William**  How?

**Hugh**  In your fever you told me.

**William**  In my fever I was remarkably communicative.

**Hugh**  You were. Remarkably so.

67

**William**  You are remarkably proficient in English.

**Hugh**  I am.

**William**  Your master has taught you well.

**Hugh**  He did not teach me. I was not unfamiliar with your language. I came from a family that valued learning. I also have much Latin and more Greek.

**William**  I don't.

**Hugh**  I know.

**William**  Speak to me in your language. Sing to me.

**Hugh**  That is not possible.

**William**  Sing – speak to me in your own language.

**Hugh**  You are hearing my own language. When the English destroyed us and our tribe, we made a vow. We had lost power to govern our lives and part of that curse was the loss we accepted over the government of our tongue. We do not break our vows. I will not sing nor speak to you in Irish, Englishman.

**William**  I can speak a little Italian. I've been there.

**Hugh**  The heart of Popery.

**William**  But the wine is excellent. (*William drinks.*)

**Hugh**  Do you come to this country with an army?

**William**  No. Only a few of us ventured the crossing. Actors, mostly. Very foolhardy. Where are they now? I know not. Why do you think the English are in Ireland?

**Hugh**  Some say we were there for the taking, others say it is to save our souls. There is a suspicion that you wish to turn us into the greatest shire of England, and there are others who whisper that the desire for blood drives your race forward. I, being an intelligent man, reject all such simplicities.

**William**  So what do you believe?

**Hugh**  I have heard word that the English are trying to grow vines in parts of Donegal. I guess they have come here for the drink.

**William**  And do the Irish drink?

**Hugh**  No. (*Hugh drinks.*)

**William**  You've lied.

**Hugh**  Beautifully.

**William**  To beauty.

*William drinks. He offers Hugh the jug. Hugh declines.*

Why do you serve Edmund?

**Hugh**  He instructs me in the art of winning.

**William**  Are you a traitor to your countrymen?

**Hugh**  I have ceased to have countrymen. I am a servant to the crown. I am a servant's servant. I am too humble to have a country. I am the lowest of the low, but like you, I wish to serve, I wish to learn.

**William**  Do you have a wife?

**Hugh**  I have had women.

**William**  Edmund's wife, have you had her?

**Hugh**  Elizabeth?

**William**  Elizabeth.

*Light on Elizabeth and the File who have resumed sewing.*

69

**Elizabeth**  How gentle the house is.

**File**  How lovely the house is.

*They smile.*

**Hugh**  Why do you ask me that?

**William**  I wish to know.

**Hugh**  And would you tell?

**William**  I might. The servant cuckolds the master. It is the stuff of comedy.

**Hugh**  Were it true, I would be hung by the neck until I died. Would you find my hanging the stuff of comedy? Have you seen a hanging?

**William**  I have seen a burning.

**Hugh**  Who?

**William**  Heretics. Catholics.

*Silence.*

**Elizabeth**  How did your child die?

**File**  In my arms.

*Silence.*

**William**  A woman screaming at the stake. They'd shaved her bald. I could see her skull. Her breasts were not like breasts any more. (*He drinks, chokes, spits out wine, it stains his shirt.*) I stood observing. My heart turned cold. I heard her voice on fire. I could not put it out. I would have turned my head away from the horror but for the fear I might have been mistaken for a weeping relative and branded with this burning woman. I kept my eyes firmly set on her suffering. The stench of her flesh corrupted me. I grew cruel in that instant.

*Silence.*

**File** They took the child. (*Silence.*) The child was taken from me. It had been snowing heavily that night. We were hiding in the mountains. We had lost our homes. We trooped across the hills, seeking any sanctuary. So many of us at first. As I was with child, I was not expected to survive. I did. It did not, the child. We buried it in the snow. It now has melted, of course. The snow, the child. I was called upon to weep. I did not do so. Instead I was determined from that moment to join with the English. We had lost. You had won. I decided to serve the winning side.

**Elizabeth** Why do you not hate us?

**File** I do not hate you.

**Elizabeth** Nor I you.

**File** Then it's settled.

**Elizabeth** Yes.

*They continue sewing.*

**Hugh** I have only once seen a hanging. It was a child. The mother twisted its neck. It was my child. I watched it happen. I let it happen. We were hiding in the mountains, seeking any sanctuary. So many of us. Dashed its brains out, she did. She had sworn to survive. It didn't, the child. Spilt like milk on the winter snow.

**William** A tale indeed that's best for winter.

**Hugh** She saw me weep that once, only that once.

*Silence.*

**File** Your husband is in great distress.

**Elizabeth** I cannot relieve it.

**File** He locks himself away. The work of administration

he ignores. His zeal diminishes into nothing. He is ceasing –

**Elizabeth**  To do as the crown dictates him to do.

**File**  He will be recalled.

**Elizabeth**  Aye, that is a smart surmise.

**File**  In disgrace, perhaps.

**Elizabeth**  What is disgrace at home compared to sorrow in exile?

**File**  You said you had come to love this country.

**Elizabeth**  But I would live in my own.

**File**  You should help your husband. Hear his distress.

**Elizabeth**  You may do so.

**File**  With your consent?

**Elizabeth**  My command.

**File**  As you wish.

**Elizabeth**  As I wish.

*The File exits. Fade on Elizabeth.*

**William**  I have a child that dies as well. A son.

**Hugh**  Then we are men without children.

**William**  I have daughters. They are alive and healthy. Yes, I have lost a son.

**Hugh**  Did you weep?

*Silence.*

**William**
Farewell, thou art too dear for my possessing,
And like enough thou know'st thy estimate.

The charter of thy worth gives thee releasing.
My bonds in thee are all determinate.
For how do I hold thee but by thy granting?
And for that riches where is my deserving?
The cause of this fair gift in me is wanting,
And so my patent back again is swerving.
Thy self thou gavest – thy self thou gavest –
Thy self thou gavest –

**Hugh**  Thy own worth then not knowing –

**William**
Thy own worth then not knowing,
Or me to whom thou gavest, else mistaking,
So thy great gift upon misprison growing,
Comes home again, in better judgement making.
Thus have I had thee as a dream doth flatter:
In sleep a king, but waking, no such matter.

*Silence.*

My legal, lawful son, no doubt about it, I assure you.

*Hugh's bare foot moves towards William's bare foot.*
*Their feet touch and rest together.*

He haunts me. He returns, demanding vengeance, my son.

**Hugh**  What for?

**William**  For being born to die. He returns in dreams to
avenge his birth, the son against the father. I think he
wishes to kill me.

**Hugh**  And will he?

**William**  I will see to it I kill him first.

**Hugh**  He is already dead.

**William**  The dead can rise.

**Hugh**  Only in dreams.

**William**  Yes. Goodnight.

**Hugh**  Waking, no such matter.

**William**  No. Goodnight.

**Hugh**  You know why the File thinks the English are in Ireland? To bring you.

**William**  Then she is a fool.

**Hugh**  Perhaps.

*Hugh leaves William to sit in silence. From his pocket William takes a child's toy. He cradles it and sings.*

**William**
Your cat's asleep before the fire.
Wonder, child, what does it see,
There are no powers that are higher,
Lord, what fools we mortals be.

The cat, it plots to steal the cream
And holds its putrid, perfumed breath.
Sweet child, it's all but strangest dreams
Until they end in darkest death.

A black cat speaks to me at times
And makes my art a witch of craft.
I call that cat by your soft name,
And then I hear the spirits laugh.

*He pats the earth gently with the doll. The storm is nearly at its height. The File begins to hear William and inch towards him.*

Come, ye spirits, come. I call the poets of this house to speak as I declare. I call on them to serve my soul as I am their superior. File, gain the gift. Edmund, by my voice are you possessed. Servant of the queen receive my spite, be my servant. (*William throws some wine on the earth.*)

There's magic in the web of it.
There's magic in the web of it.

*William traces patterns with the spilt wine. The storm is
at its height.*

My soul doth magnify my Lord.
And my spirit rejoiceth.

*The File and Edmund enter, possessed by William's
spell.*

My soul doth magnify my Lord,
And my spirit rejoiceth.
Lovers, to bed, 'tis almost time. Kneel.

*They kneel before him. The storm ceases. Music.
William blesses the heads of the File and Edmund with
wine.*

Rise, ye spirits, from your graves,
Come ye from cold mountain caves.
Fear not light nor tender morn,
Here the night be charmed and horned.
Dreams ye dared of dark desires,
Forged in passion's funeral pyres.
Ye have got no souls to save.
Rise, ye spirits, from the grave.

I call upon
An ancient quarrel.

**File**
Greece and Troy,
Troy besieged. Troy, desolate.

**William**
Say, poet, if you practised
The art of war –

**Edmund**

In that sore bloodshed –

**File**

Where neighbour against neighbour
Did raise a savage claw and rip flesh from flesh.

*Music. The Irish appear before them to perform the*
*Fall of Troy. Maeve plays Hecuba, Annas plays*
*Cassandra, Sweney plays Priam, Donal and Niall play*
*his sons.*

I call upon
The broken towers of Troy, Troy
That fell, Troy most desolate. Say,
If you hear my lament,
For I would roar from bloodstained ruins
The secrets my poor people
Spilt on to the shores and shadows of the earth.
Kind Hecuba,
And wise Cassandra,
Priam and his sons,
Assemble here to weave the thread of your saga.

I call upon
The broken towers of Troy, Troy
That fell, Troy most desolate. Say,
Hecuba, if eyes see,
If ears hear, how would they now attend
To what your two eyes and ears
Did witness when the gods abandoned Troy
To cruel fate,
When murder followed
Priam and his sons.
Speak if you have words to tell, loosen thy tied tongue.

**Hecuba**

I, Hecuba,

Mother of my tribe, for mercy's
Sake, did make my moan, on bended knee
Did seek forgiveness, mercy
For my sons and daughters. Hard laughter
Struck me in the face and
The sea itself, I heard it weep wild tears for
Lost Hecuba,
Ravished Cassandra,
Priam and his sons.
I heard the winds that scraped our skin sing our saga.

You, Cassandra,
Daughter of our tribe, for mercy's
Sake who made your moan, on bended knee
Who sought forgiveness, now keen
Our name throughout the earth, desolate
And in shadow, in sorrow,
Beat your wild tears against the sky, break the moon
That lights your mother;
She'd die in darkness.
Priam and his sons,
Where they have fallen, know nothing of rest.

Cassandra
I, Cassandra,
Did foretell the broken towers
Of Troy, Troy most desolate. Sour
Were my words of warning,
But I will bless the bloodstained ruins
And drink dry the sea's wild tears
Spilt, remembering my Father. Remember
Me, my mother,
Most loved Hecuba,
Priam and his sons.
Assemble here to sound the song of your saga.

**Priam** (*sings*)
Our spirits rise from out their graves
And come from the cold mountain caves.
Better a man not to be born
Than face Night that's charmed and horned.

*His Sons sing.*

**Sons**
Dreams we dared of dark desire
That were forged in funeral pyres
Have left us no souls to save.
Our spirits rise from out their graves.

*The Women sing.*

**Women**
My soul doth magnify my Lord.
He gave to me the bitter word.
The child you bear will pass as dust.
Their power is mortal, their lives cursed.
Chaos of change that none can flee,
This earth is Mutabilitie.
Where lies a man there hangs time's sword.
My soul doth magnify my Lord.

*The Irish sing in chorus.*

**Irish**
Great Gloriana, learn from Troy,
Your kingdom's but a paltry toy.
Great Gloriana, none are saved
When spirits rise from out their graves.

*The Irish move towards Edmund.*

**Edmund** Out of every corner of the woods and glens they came creeping forth upon their hands, for their legs could not bear them.

*Light on Elizabeth and the sleeping children. Elizabeth cries out in her sleep.*

**Elizabeth**  Husband.

**Edmund**  They looked like anatomies of death.

*A Child cries out in its sleep.*

**Child**  Father.

**Edmund**  They spoke like ghosts crying out of their graves.

*Another Child cries out.*

**Child**  Father.

**Edmund**  In such short space there were none almost left. In all that war, there perished not many by the sword but all by the extremity of famine.

*The Irish scream in unison to him.*

**Irish**  Father, father, father.

**Edmund**  Fire, fire.

*The Irish vanish. His screams waken his family.*

**Elizabeth**  Edmund.

**Edmund**  Let me have fire to see what demons haunt me.

*Edmund clings to Elizabeth.*

I have seen my late father in these wars of Munster. He is a frightened child fleeing through the hills. He is hungry for food and I refuse him bread. The fires of hell leap about his feet and he runs away from me so quickly. Father, I will burn my books. I will burn my house. I will flee with you, father.

*Edmund races away, followed by his family. Silence.*

79

*Hugh is also awake, watching from the shadows.*

**File**
I call upon
An ancient quarrel. Greece and Troy
Troy besieged, desolate. Say,
Poet, if you practised
The art of war in that sore bloodshed
Where neighbour against neighbour
Did raise a savage claw and rip flesh from flesh.
Elizabeth,
Great queen of England,
Your name rhymes with death.

*Hugh enters.*

**Hugh**  William is not our saviour. Words will not help us. Now we know this castle inside out, and the minds of our enemies are ours for the taking.

**File**  The time is not yet right.

**Hugh**  Stay here or come with me to the forest. (*Silence. Hugh exits.*)

**File**  Elizabeth, Elizabeth, you rhyme with death.


### SCENE THREE

*The forest. Flash of light and wild music. Niall and Donal stand in strange robes in judgement over Richard and Ben, who are terrified. Their hands and feet are now cut free. The other Irish look on.*

**Niall**  Word has come to us of your treachery.

**Ben**  What treachery?

**Donal**  Have you been asked to speak?

**Ben** No.

**Donal** Then be silent.

**Niall** There is one punishment for treachery. It is beheading.

**Richard** For God's sake, girl, save us.

*Silence.*

**Niall** You have sought to defile my innocent sister –

**Ben** How the hell could he have defiled her? He's been tied up, he couldn't move. I'm his witness.

**Richard** They are going to kill us, Ben. They are going to kill us.

**Niall** Sister, make your accusation.

**Annas** He did move to me at night, good brother. He did speak most lewdly. He asked me to kiss, and I refused his mouth. He spoke then words that soured my soul. I turned away, my tears of shame streamed, but he knew no pity. His man's strength held me to the earth.

**Richard** This is a lie.

**Annas** I did try to call out against him, but my voice is a woman's cry and it was not heard.

**Richard** Lies, lies.

**Niall** This is the judgement you seek, good sister?

**Annas** Deal with him according to the dictates of our law. Let me, the violated, appoint a fair judge.

**Niall** Who do you require to pass sentence?

**Annas** His countryman, his companion.

**Richard** Save me.

**Ben** We should take our time over all of this. A man's life is at stake, as well as a lady's honour. The girl could be confused. It is so easy to mistake a flirtation for something more serious: Richard is a very good lad, a bit easy maybe, he likes his bit of hole wherever he can find it, in a manner of speaking – oh Christ, I'm making this worse. I can't judge. He should not die. He is a young man. He means no harm. Let him go. Let us go. We'll go home. We'll never bother you again. Honest to God.

**Niall** Was my sister lying?

**Ben** No, she was mistaken, that's all. It's the easiest thing in the world to make a mistake, when you're young. They're young, the two of them.

**Donal** By our laws, a life must be taken to pay for this violation. Do you offer your life for your countryman's pardon?

**Ben** Do you know this reminds me of a play I once acted in?

**Richard** I don't think they want to know about that, Ben.

**Ben** Two friends were condemned to die. A pardon came from the king for one of them. The punishment now was in their choosing which was to live. They both chose death and they were saved. The Two Thieves, that was its name. One looked to the king, and he said, my lord, my friend is to me as my breath is to my body. Were his breath to cease, so should my body cease, for my heart, heavy with woe, burdened by stones of sorrow, will shatter into a multitude of pieces, each as sharp as tears of tribulation I now shed to plead for his life. Let a miracle of mercy now attend this unhappy session, and bid my friend be free.

**Niall** He is free to live, as are you. (*He laughs.*)

**Donal** Niall, embrace them to you. Their eloquence is

worthy to be of our faith and of our breed.

*Niall holds out his open arms.*

**Ben**  No, I will not go to you.

**Niall**  Then I shall come to you.

*Niall embraces Ben.*

**Ben**  I'm a decent man. I ask only that I be allowed to leave this captivity and return to my home with my friend. If as you say I am of your breed and your faith, listen to my request and let us go. Man to man, I ask this, one equal to another.

**Niall**  This honesty moves me. Let me embrace you, Richard, and find in me a friend as true as the good woman who has spoken so wisely to us all. Good sister, forgive.

*Annas kisses Richard.*

**Annas**  Revenge.

*Richard embraces Niall. Niall stabs Richard.*

**Ben**  Richard, lad? Richard? Friend, old friend?

**Niall**  Am I fit to rule, father?

**Sweney**  You are fit to lead. There is a difference. The times demand that difference. You are my blood. I am well pleased. Lead me to the body that I may pay the respect due to the English dead.

**Donal**  My lord.

*He leads Sweney to Richard's corpse. Sweney bathes his hands in Richard's blood. He holds out his bloodied hands.*

**Sweney**  My wife?

*Maeve goes to him and kisses his hands.*

My children?

*Annas and Niall kneel before him.*

My priest?

**Donal**  My lord?

*Sweney smears Annas's and Niall's faces with blood. As he does so, Donal incants.*

Do this in memory of me. Do this in memory of me.

*Sweney points to Ben.*

Do this in memory of me.

**Sweney**  Do as I command you. Kill him. Kill them all.

*Wild music. Ben squeals like an animal, crying out finally, 'William, save me, save me.' They surround him. He charges wildly about them. He falls to the earth, crying as they knife him, then hauling him and Richard off.*

# Act Five

## SCENE ONE

*The castle. Edmund nurses his child.*

**Edmund**  You must be very quiet. Do you promise to be very quiet?

**Child**  Yes, father.

**Edmund**  Quiet as a mouse. Quiet as a cat catching a mouse. Promise to be quiet.

**Child**  Yes, father.

**Edmund**  Why do you call me father?

**Child**  Because you are my father.

**Edmund**  I too had a father. He is dead. Pray for him. I want to ask you something. Will you be my father?

**Child**  I can't be. You are my father.

**Edmund**  If you do not obey me, then I will kill you, and I will know for sure you are dead, father, you will stay in your grave this time.

   *Edmund's hands go to the Child's throat.*

**Child**  Father. (*The Child struggles.*) Father, you are hurting me. (*The Child screams.*) Father.

   *Edmund releases the Child. The Child looks in terror at Edmund.*

**Edmund**  We were playing cat and mouse. (*Silence.*) You were not quiet. (*Silence.*) Cat and mouse, yes?

**Child**  I hate you, father.

85

*The Child runs off. Music, a distorted reprise of 'The Song of Common Prayer'.*

**Edmund** (*sings*)
This song we sing of common prayer
Decrees we stand in your true faith.


SCENE TWO

*The forest.*

**Donal**  My lord, the trace of English blood becomes you, great warrior.

**Niall**  Our enemies wait in terror of us.

**Donal**  Your people shall scatter them in your name.

**Niall**  Give but the word and they will gather before the fortress of the English and raze it to the ground. Our father, our king, your sons will defend you from peril of death.

**Sweney**  I have no stomach for a fight. I wish to lie in earth that is consecrated only by the rain, and blessed by the wind. I am no longer fit to be your father, let alone your king.

*There is a burst of birdsong.*

How wisely the birds sing. I am beginning to understand their song. These creatures of the sun are kind. They seek to lift my heart. Even old men can envy the flight of birds. Good birds, you know nothing of a kingdom lost. You are kings of sky and stars, I am lord of river and forest, but river and forest do not heed my command. Shall these kind birds heed me? Answer me this, my friends. Why is it a man can walk and talk, can run and reason, but cannot fly? Is he afraid? I am not. What must I do? Jump higher

86

and higher? (*He gets to his feet and jumps.*) Higher? Jump higher?

*He tries to jump higher and falls. Niall and Donal rush to lift him. Sweney roars imperiously.*

Back, dogs, back. Do not dare lay hands upon your king. He has fallen, but he will rise. He will fly.

*As Sweney raises himself with difficulty, Hugh enters and kneels before his father.*

I have been asking how a man can fly. Jumping high is no answer. (*He skips jerkily.*) I fly. (*He skips again.*) I fly.

**Maeve** Good, kind bird, come back from the sky. Fly to my hand.

*Sweney takes Maeve's hand.*

**Sweney** I have flown through the trees down from the sky, for I saw that pretty swallow. (*He points at Annas.*) She has flown from Egypt, the sun is on her wings.

**Maeve** She wishes to see more of the forest. Will you show it to her?

*He goes to Annas.*

Daughter, walk with this gentle creature of the air.

**Annas** My father.

**Sweney** I would not be your father. Rather I'd be your pet. Build me a golden cage. I will sing for you there till your heart bursts with joy.

**Annas** Aye, father, my heart bursts.

*Sweney and Annas exit.*

**Maeve** You were asking, Niall, when the word to attack would be given. I read in your face, Hugh, that you have returned to say that that time is now. Before that word is given, I must give you my last command. It is to kill your father and myself. It is to kill your king and queen.

**Hugh** My loved mother –

**Maeve** Your queen commands her subjects to fulfil her will, and as you are my sons so you are my subjects. Raise your knives and kill us. That is the first attack. I will appoint the time and place. I must prepare our souls for death.

**Niall** Priest, speak.

**Donal** My Queen, in the name of Christ, his most holy mother, Mary –

**Maeve** We shall soon be in their arms.

**Hugh** You shall soon be in hell if this killing is to be – Mother, I beg you, such evil –

**Maeve** What is evil? (*Silence.*) Is it evil to believe yourself to be a bird? (*She laughs.*) A bird. So shall he live in a golden cage? Would that soft gold were beaten into a sharp sword to pierce his sore heart and thereby still it. Aye, we have indeed fallen from a great height. I fell, not willingly, but I had in my warrior's heart the hope to rise again –

**Niall** We shall rise again, mother.

**Maeve** Niall, you are a fool. God has turned against us. And your father, your king, will drag all your hopes into the ground with him. We two shall not rise again. That is my warning. Do you see why you must kill me?

**Niall** I will never –

**Maeve** Never? Never? Then let me live like this. I'd throw my crown to the pigs if we had pigs to trample on it. I'd grind my jewels beneath a millstone had we mills to make our bread. My heart I'd tear out of my body and feed my starving people, had I a people. Once I had a kingdom and a people, a husband and a king. Now I have nothing. No, I have a life. And a power to end it. Give your mother what she asks for.

**Hugh**  Thy will be done.

*Silence.*

**Niall**  Thy will be done.


### SCENE THREE

*Elizabeth enters.*

**Elizabeth**  I am returning to England.

**Edmund**  England, my love?

**Elizabeth**  Will you come home with me? To England?

**Edmund**  How do we abandon the castle?

**Elizabeth**  I do not care. Say they invaded it. Say it fell about our ears. Say they burned it to the ground. Do you hear me? We cannot live in a burning building. We cannot serve in the flames.

**Edmund**  Yes.

**Elizabeth**  We are ready to flee.

**Edmund**  I am returning to die in England.

**Elizabeth**  Burn this castle to the ground. (*She leaves him alone.*)

*Sweney enters, garlanded with flowers.*

**Maeve**  You have ceased to recognize me, or so I take it from your strange silence.

**Sweney**  Good maid, it is no insult to your beauty nor does strangeness affect me, but the strangeness of glimpsing what is surely a goddess sent from the heavens to delight men's eyes.

**Maeve**  Would you ask me my name?

**Sweney**  It is Aphrodite, for I have been taught she is the loveliest of all divinities.

**Maeve**  Who taught you so?

**Sweney**  My tutors in Greek and Latin.

**Maeve**  Your father must be a rich man to provide such instruction.

**Sweney**  He is a king.

**Maeve**  As is mine.

**Sweney**  I know.

**Maeve**  How?

**Sweney**  My father told me so.

**Maeve**  As my father told me who you were.

**Sweney**  We then are known to each other.

**Maeve**  We met as children. I was ever the warrior, even then. I played roughly with you. I made you cry and did comfort you, lovely boy.

**Sweney**  Soft boy, that's what you called me. I have not forgotten.

**Maeve**  Lie in my arms.

**Sweney**  I long to, but I am a young man, not long versed in the art of love.

**Maeve**  There is no art to love. There is an art in asking. I practise that art. I ask you for love.

**Sweney**  As I ask you.

*They embrace.*

My father the king speaks well of you.

**Maeve**  My father the king speaks well of you.

**Sweney**  My mother the queen speaks well of you.

**Maeve**  My mother the queen speaks well of you. My hound barks well of you, the horse neighs well of you, the birds in golden cages sing well of you, so all in all I hoped to find you well spoken. And well spoken you are, my scholar.

**Sweney**  My wife? Will you be my wife?

**Maeve**  My husband.

**Sweney**  We shall have children, sons and daughters to fill the earth, a hundred sons and daughters –

**Maeve**  A hundred? I'm not quite sure –

**Sweney**  It has happened in history before, my tutors assure me. The King of Troy had a hundred sons and daughters.

**Maeve**  Troy?

**Sweney**  A city that fell to Greece. We shall never fall. We shall grow and build an empire founded on our love.

**Maeve**  Aye, we shall, my husband, I remember.

**Sweney**  You are too young to remember.

**Maeve**  With these same words you wooed me.

**Sweney**  Too young, too young.

**Maeve**  I have grown too young to remember.

**Sweney**  My blood is hot with love of you.

**Maeve**  Scholar, you are growing into a man learned in love.

**Sweney**  Let's steal to bed and learn some more.

**Maeve**  Let us prepare our souls. Let us say our prayers.

**Sweney**  I do not wish to pray.

**Maeve**  You must. A prayer of thanksgiving, my husband, to each other.

**Sweney**  How shall we give thanks to each other in prayer?

*She kisses him.*

I do return your thanks.

*He kisses her.*

**Maeve**  To bed, to bed.

*She leads him out.*


### SCENE FIVE

*The river.*

**William**  I follow the river and it leads to a port?

**File**  Yes. Goodbye.

**William** You barely speak to me, yet I gave you what you asked for. Did you not like my gift?

**File** You are a fearful creature, William. It is only in delirium you acquire the strength to sing. And your gift was a dream, a fantasy. A man shall come from the river, a Bard of Avon, to sing the song of songs and save us. There is no such song, is there? (*Silence.*) I believed in the wrong man, you didn't exist. (*Silence.*) Do you not exist? Did you ever exist? And if you do not, then do I? Am I nothing? Is there nothing? Tell me, help me, William.

**William** How?

**File** Let me believe in you, even if you're not the truth.

**William** No.

**File** I will die without faith. My people will die. They have lost all except faith. Let us keep it.

**William** Keep it. Stay faithful. You say your people have lost and mine have won. I am with the loser, but I won't live with them. I am going home. It is time to greet the loved soil of England again. Once as a boy I ran all the way from home to the great city of London. It was from your faith I was running – I don't believe it. The journey there was hard and now I must make another hard journey. I am looking forward to it, I swear. I do believe in the journey, for I had made it myself, that and all I imagined.

**File** You are yourself what you imagined, as I am what I imagined. That is your gift to me. I have to accept it.

**William** Do you not want it? (*Silence.*) I have a living to make. I do exist but not as you imagined. Another crooked sixpence in a crooked house among men as crooked as myself.

**File** In London?

**William**  Where I found another faith –

**File**  The faith you do believe in. Live, give life. (*Silence.*) Find that faith here. Stay with me, give life in Ireland. (*Silence.*) Priest.

**William**  Poet. Haste you to the forest.

**File**  Haste you to England.

**William**  Fear the fire.

**File**  I fear you.

**William**  And I you.

> *Their hands touch. He is gone. The File sings.*

**File**
> When I was a child,
> A little child,
> I did believe in God and man,
> But God and man,
> God and man . . .

> *There is silence, broken by a caw of birds. Annas enters with the File.*

**Annas**  We have fallen from a great height, File. Shall we ever rise again? He did believe he had turned into a winged creature. He asked me to place him into a golden cage. Would that soft gold were beaten into a sharp sword to pierce my sore heart and thereby still it.

> *Donal enters, followed by Hugh and Niall, their knives bloodied. Silence.*

**Hugh**  They did command us.

> *Silence.*

**File**  My lord, my lady, my life.

*The File races off. Annas screams, attacking her brothers, who try to calm her. Failing, Hugh violently subdues her. She lies on the earth, weeping.*

**Hugh** Our father had abandoned reason and our mother had abandoned life. She prayed to us to end their days. Do you think I heard that prayer with an easy heart? Stone itself would melt to hear her plea of sorrow.

**Annas** Aye, stone would melt. Ice would melt. But my brothers hardened to their task. They turned the very source of life into dead stone and ice. From this day forward all hearts be the same stone and ice. Old men and women will be murdered in their beds by those they call their children, their strong sons, who kill their loving flesh and blood to show their courage. Courage? No, curse instead. I curse you.

**Hugh** Lift your curse. It will be heard, Annas. Do not damn us.

**Annas** You have damned yourself. You have damned my soul for cursing you. You have killed us all, brother.

**Hugh** When I did strike the blow, I knew I'd lost my soul. My father and mother – my father and my mother – at peace, asleep, I wished them peace. My king and my queen, I wished to do as they commanded, I acted in awe and obedience – I did as they demanded, my king and my queen.

*The File enters.*

My mother and my father – I have killed my mother and my father. Do not look on me.

**Niall** I watched and did not still his hand. I let him spill their sacred blood.

**Annas** They say they did as our mother bid.

**Donal**  I did hear my lady beg for death.

**Annas**  And priest, you did not answer?

*Silence.*

**Niall**  You would take our lives, sister?

**Annas**  You will take your own lives, and I will go with you to meet our maker, for by my own hand I too will die.

**Niall**  There is a war to fight.

**Annas**  The war you fight is over. You have stained your hands with holy blood. They are stained with blood for ever. From this day forward your war against the English will fail.

**Hugh**  I kept my counsel in the Englishman's castle. I worked as his slave to learn his ways and tactics. I let the File madden him and his wife until they were children in her care, ready for the taking. Now is our moment. Must I now lose victory for our race through your command to die?

**Annas**  I command you as my father and mother, our king and queen, did command you with absolute authority for you are not fit to follow in the issuing of a command. Die.

**Hugh**  File, plead for my life. (*Silence.*) Plead for my life. (*Silence.*) In the name of our lost love, I plead you, save my life. (*Silence.*) I plead in the name of our lost child.

**File**  I knelt where my lord and lady loved arm-in-arm in death. I kissed their hands and feet. I saw the light of eternal rest in their faces. The grave itself did weep, and in that weeping I heard their sweet voices speak. They say, repent, repent for your revenge. Leave the world and its desires. Renounce the kingdom. Walk as beggars through the earth. Or there is no consolation beyond the grave. Repent. Be penitent. Be pilgrims.

**Annas** Well, priest, what do you say is God's will in this? (*Silence.*) Silence? Is that God's will? So be it. Eternal silence guide us. My brothers, will you follow me and renounce the world?

**Hugh** Scatter our followers, let them haste away.

**Donal** My lord, they wait for your instruction –

**Hugh** That is my instruction, priest. Follow it.

**Donal** That is my thanks and reward for all my service? Walk as a beggar through the earth? I do so now. My vestments are rags. You must not listen to the cries of women. Restore me to glory, great king, if you so make yourself. Drink the warrior blood of your dead. Restore the order of our laws, our customs, our religion. Through your power, your valour, and through prayer – prayer – through prayer – through faith – we will win – we will – through God –

**Hugh** Poor priest, look at you. Look at us. We are nothing. My sister, I will live with you in eternal destitution. My brother, will you walk with us?

**Niall** I will never desert you.

**Hugh** Nor I you.

**Annas** My family is my fate.

**Donal** I have loved you all my life, and will not cease to love.

**File** Nor will I cease to love.

*Annas, Niall and Donal leave.*

**Hugh** Nor have I ceased to love.

**File** My heart hardened when I lost the child.

**Hugh** So I wished it.

**File**  Then wish it back to life now.

**Hugh**  I do.

**File**  I do.

**Hugh**  Our journey begins.

**File**  It begins.


## SCENE SIX

*Edmund is alone.*

**Edmund**  All children should die before their father dies.
That way they may not stain their pretty feet in the pool
of foul and filthy sin. Father, forgive me, I have failed.
Failed. My wife and children are not abed. They stand
prepared to flee from you, my castle built into the air.
Shall you vanish after me into wreck and ruin? You shel-
tered me from rain and snow. I now abandon you to this
afflicted country. I should wish you stand for ever, but
what have these senseless stones done to deserve such
infection as eternal life? Eternal life, eternal light – such
illusions of the mind, the broken, battered mind, torn to
ribbons on the rack of its confusion. I did my best, these
dumb walls cry in all innocence. Indeed you did. Indeed
you did. But you could not succeed, for I fashioned you
from my broken mind, your masonry is my lost majesty,
and yet the mind may be mended. Perhaps these stones
are not senseless. They are capable of crime. Crime
against my person, crime against my country. This is high
treason. I must sentence you, my castle, to severest punishment. As we do burn heretic flesh, so I must burn
heretic stone. You, my great cathedral, where my queen
was virgin goddess, have turned to devil worship. I must
free the devil from you and baptize you anew in fire.

Cleansed, these stones will be free. Fire, burn. Fire. Fire.

*Edmund flees. Fire.*


### SCENE SEVEN

*A river. The Irish move with a new freedom. Hugh bathes in the river, watched by the File. Annas and Donal prepare a frugal meal. What clothes cover them do so with ease.*

**File**  I do not approve of a man who takes so long to bathe. It shows signs of vanity.

*Hugh makes no response.*

Apart from your vanity you are quite perfect, and I dislike perfection.

**Hugh**  No, you don't.

**File**  You are the vainest man I know.

**Hugh**  Bathe with me.

**File**  No.

*Hugh drenches her with water. She drenches him back. They caress each other with water. Hugh dresses.*

Do you miss the life before?

**Hugh**  I think of it.

**File**  So do I.

**Hugh**  Shall we return to it?

**File**  And defy your dying father?

**Hugh**  Is his blood washed off my hands? (*He shows her his hands.*)

**File**  They are clean.

**Hugh**  So may I kill again?

*Niall enters, leading a bedraggled, terrified Child by the hand.*

**Niall**  Look what the forest has found.

*Silence. The Child recognizes the File and Hugh.*

**Child**  Are you our servants?

**Hugh**  Aye, your servants.

**Child**  You were kind.

**File**  Kind.

**Annas**  Why are you lost in the forest, child?

**Child**  Our castle caught fire. Bad men must have done it. Our father was laughing. Our mother could not get him to leave. I was frightened of the flames. They looked like hell. I ran away. Then they were gone. They must have thought me dead in the fire. I was only hiding. They didn't know I was alive. I tried to follow them but I got lost. And I've found you. File, what's wrong? Are you frightened?

**File**  Yes, I'm frightened.

**Child**  Did I frighten you? I'm very sorry.

**File**  I'm very sorry too.

**Annas**  We have a child.

**Niall**  An English child.

**Donal**  A hostage.

**Hugh**  We have a child. He is to be fostered as our own. Reared as our own. Nurtured like our own, and natured like his own, as decreed by our laws, our customs, our religion.

**Child**  I am hungry, I could eat a horse, Hugh.

**Annas**  Our bill of fare does not stretch to horse, but there are berries and meat and sweet herbs and water to drink.

**Hugh**  There is milk.

**Donal**  There is little.

**File**  Fetch our little milk.

*Annas fetches milk and the Child takes it from her.*

Drink the milk.

*The Child drinks the milk.*

Eat.

*They sit and eat. Music.*